Diana Sweeney was born in Auckland and moved to Sydney at the age of twelve. She now lives in northern New South Wales.

the minnow
diana sweeney

TEXT PUBLISHING MELBOURNE AUSTRALIA

textpublishing.com.au

The Text Publishing Company
Swann House
22 William Street
Melbourne Victoria 3000
Australia

First published in Australia by The Text Publishing Company 2014

Cover and page design by Imogen Stubbs
Cover illustration by Katie Harnett
Typeset by J&M Typesetters

Printed in Australia by Griffin Press, an Accredited ISO AS/NZS 14001:2004 Environmental Management System printer.

National Library of Australia Cataloguing-in-Publication entry
Author: Sweeney, Diana.
Title: The minnow / by Diana Sweeney.
ISBN: 9781922182012 (paperback)
ISBN: 9781925095012 (ebook)
Subjects: Bildungsromans.
              Grief—Juvenile fiction.
Dewey Number: A823.4

for Mum

1

'I think Bill is in love with Mrs Peck,' I confide to an under-sized blue swimmer crab that has become all tangled up in my line. The little crab doesn't appear to be the slightest bit interested, so I finish pulling it free and toss it over the side of Bill's dinghy. It makes a plopping sound as it enters the water and I watch it swim away. Bill, as usual, is asleep. He sleeps with his hand dangling over the edge, the line tied to his little finger. Sometimes I have to kick him awake, although he swears he always feels the fish tugging. That's Bill. Bit of a liar.

I live with Bill in the boatshed at Jessops Creek. I moved in after the Mother's Day flood. I'm used to it now, but I missed my old room at first. Nana says you get used to anything if you've got enough time. She says she still misses Papa—my grandfather—even though he died before I was born. I keep a photo of Papa next to my bed. Nana gave it to me after the flood. She said Papa would keep me company. She said he had been doing such a fine job of keeping her company over the years, she was sure he had special powers. Nana lives at the Mavis Ornstein Home for the Elderly. She has given photos of Papa to everyone there.

I sleep in the loft. It's small, but perfect for me. It used to be Bill's bedroom, but the ceiling is really low so I don't think he minded moving downstairs. When I asked him about it, he just shrugged and said headroom was highly overrated.

I totally disagree. My old bedroom had lots of head-room. I could stand on the bedside table with my arms outstretched and still not reach the ceiling. Now, if I stand up really straight, the top of my head already touches the beam. If I keep growing I'll have to bend my neck. I often think about that headroom. I miss it.

Instead of windows, the loft has large double doors that open onto the roof. They're closed during the day to keep out the heat, but at night, with them propped wide open, I can watch the sky. One of the old ladies at Nana's home gave me her astronomy chart when I told her about my stargazing. She said 'such enthusiasm should be nurtured'. Her name is Mavis;

she is ninety-eight, and she thinks the home is named after her. She also thinks Papa is her late husband. Nana said she almost regretted giving a photo to Mavis until she realised it was just another example of Papa's special powers. Mavis was happy, Nana said. Why spoil it with the truth?

There is a flash of silver near my line, so I keep my hand steady and my body still, willing the fish towards the bait. Bill yawns loudly. I ignore him. Bill hates to be watched as he wakes.

'Not much is happening,' he says.

Bill has a beard, and his arms and legs are thick with hair. He always jokes that no one ever got sunburnt wearing a fur coat and, generally speaking, he's right. But today he has forgotten his cap and his nose and forehead are quite red.

'Your face has copped it,' I say, without a trace of smugness.

I always wear a long-sleeved shirt and a hat when I'm outside. It was one of Mum's rules.

The last time I saw Sarah she was floating head down with her arms and legs out from her sides like a star fish. I watched her from the roof of the fire station, counting the seconds. She held the record at fifty-two. I counted to sixty as she disappeared around the side of the newsagent. I remember thinking she was probably sneaking a breath.

Bill and I usually fish from the pier, where the fish come in only two sizes: dinner-for-four or not-worth-it. We always let the little ones go. Bill says it's one of the laws of fishing. But I feel sorry for the ones that get thrown back, swimming around with a hole through their lip (or worse).

'I think it's kinder to keep them and eat them,' I said to Bill, once.

'Don't put a hook on your line if it bothers you so much,' Bill snarled back. Sometimes Bill can be mean.

When it's too windy at the pier, we fish down at Crabs Gully. It takes ages to get there. Bill says Crabs Gully is one of the Seven Wonders of the World because it's a wonder we ever make it out alive. Ha ha.

There are heaps of blowholes at Crabs Gully, so we usually get soaked-to-misery. Soaked-to-misery is one of Nana's favourite sayings. She has a particular hankering for cold and wet situations and loves to say stuff like, 'the shivers are no match for Bovril' or 'you can't stay miserable on a full belly'.

Bill doesn't understand Nana's sayings.

Anyway, by the time we make it back to the boatshed I'm usually so cold my teeth are chattering. Bill always lights the pot-belly, then we eat soup till we burst. Bill only ever eats soup. He says he can't see the point of anything else. Nana reckons his teeth are probably crook.

Some days Bill and I catch the bus into town. Bill always needs new line and I like to look around at stuff. The best shop in town is Mingin's Hardware and Disposals.

'Hi, Bill,' says Mrs Peck.

'Why, I believe you've had your hair done, Mrs Peck,' says Bill in a voice he never uses with me. Mrs Peck flicks her head. 'And is that a new dress?' Bill continues, all smooth and soothing, like maybe he wants to see her naked.

'I'm going to look at the sinkers,' I say to no one in particular, because no one in particular is listening. I love sinkers. I love to feel their weight in my hand. It amazes me that something so small can be so heavy. Bill says gold is even heavier. I can't imagine.

Bill's hand is moving under Mrs Peck's dress. I slip a number-four sinker into my pocket and move over to the tackle boxes. You'd have to be mighty serious about fishing to want a tackle box. I stop in front of the FishMaster Super Series. It comprises three layers that concertina for ease of access. It says that on the lid. I don't usually use the word 'comprises', but I think it sounds just right. I open it. It's got a separate lock-up storage compartment for sharps and a see-through sinker box. If you buy the deluxe model you get the sinker box for free. I've never owned a tackle box. Bill and I only ever take a roll of line, a dozen hooks, a few sinkers and a knife. Bill reckons anything more is window dressing. Sometimes we buy worms, but usually we collect cabbage off the rocks. The fish love it. I've gotten most of my sinkers from Mingin's Hardware and Disposals.

Bill is pushing himself against Mrs Peck's hip. I should tell you I don't like Mrs Peck. She has an ugly grouper's mouth which she paints bright red and she makes a dry clicking sound when she speaks. She has a horrible habit of wetting her lips with her tongue, something she does at the end of every sentence. I try not to look.

Right now, she's pushing her tongue into Bill's ear, pretending for all she's worth to be absorbed in his attentions. In actual fact, she is monitoring my every move. The only time she takes her eyes off me is to glance at the door—probably checking for Mr Peck—meanwhile, Bill has his back to the world and nothing to lose.

They've decided to move away from the counter. Bill leads Mrs Peck over to the paint aisle. It's near the back of the shop, which gives them time to finish up if a customer comes in. Mrs Peck's son arrived once. Bill pretended to check the colour chart while Mrs Peck was on her knees. 'G'day Junior,' Bill called out to the kid, all casual, but keeping his hand hard on Mrs Peck's head until he was done. Sometimes Mrs Peck climbs the paint ladder and Bill stands under her dress. I have a Swiss Army knife that I got the day Bill had

Mrs Peck on her back in the Deluxe Family Weekender. Mr Peck was on a buying trip and Mrs Peck had thrown caution to the wind. 'Here you are, Tom,' she'd said, pushing a small red box into my hand. 'Be sure to check all its features.' Click, click.

The Swiss Army knife has everything: three knives, a pair of scissors, a toothpick, a bottle opener, a fish scaler, a nail cleaner and a small file that fits easily into the keyhole on the side of Mingin's register. I would have liked some coins to buy a Coke, but the change would have rattled against the sinker in my pocket, so I grabbed a lobster—that's slang for a twenty.

I'm poring over the catalogue when Bill and Mrs Peck reappear.

'Next time, I'm going to tie you up,' Bill whispers to Mrs Peck as she hands him a brand new roll of line. I make a throat-clearing sound.

'I'd like that,' Mrs Peck purrs, ignoring me. I imagine her lip all torn and bloody as I pull a rusty hook from her mouth.

'Thanks for the supplies,' Bill calls over his shoulder as we leave the shop. 'Hungry?' he asks me.

Martha's Grill is Bill's favourite spot for lunch, which is lucky because I like it too. I order the fisherman's breakfast and Bill orders the soup of the day. Martha is young and handsome and not really Martha. The real Martha sold up when her husband died, but everyone in town just went on calling the new owner Martha, even though he's nothing like Martha at all. I'm too young to remember much about the old Martha, I'm just telling you what I know.

After Martha's Grill, we head to the public pool on Cooper-Brian Street. In order to swim, you have to have a shower first. The boatshed doesn't have a shower, so the pool's amenities come in quite handy. I'm never happier than when I've had a shower, a swim and a fisherman's breakfast, and Bill's at his best after a good workout with Mrs Peck.

After the flood, some of the older folk formed the Mother's Day Survivors, and they've met every Tuesday night ever since. Christmas day fell on a Tuesday last year and the place was packed. Bill and I went, even though we're not official members. No one seemed to mind. I often wish I'd known how to fish before the flood. I could have pushed hooks through everyone's mouths and tied the lines to the roof of the fire station.

Most nights it starts to rain about midnight. Just soft spits, not enough to wake me. Before the weather changed it used to be drier than Mrs Peck's mouth. The ground was hard and dusty. Grass never grew on the oval, and Mum's flowers always died out the front. We used to swim in the neighbour's dam when it got really hot.

'Are you fishing or wishing?' Bill asks me when there's a tug on my line.

It's a little catfish. Far too undersized to keep. As I unhook it, I think of my sister floating away, her head under the water looking at the things in the sea. The catfish asks me what I'm doing, its little mouth mouthing the words.

'I'm throwing you back, Sarah,' I say. 'You belong in the water now, and I belong here with Bill.'

'Have you had sex yet?' she asks. But I can't answer because Bill is watching me talk to a fish and I feel stupid.

The answer is yes, if you must know. I had sex a few weeks ago. It happened unexpectedly, after a Martha's breakfast, at the public pool. I was in the change room, stripping off my wet boardies when Bill walked in. 'Tom,' Bill said, staring at me, mouth gapping, 'you're a *girl*.'

My name hasn't always been Tom. It used to be Tomboy and before that it was Holly. Even Nana calls me Tom. I've been Tom so long, even if I changed back to Holly, no one would take any notice—look at poor Martha. So, for almost a year, living in the boatshed, Bill thought I was a boy. Maybe he wouldn't have taken me in, if he had known I was a girl.

Anyway, we mucked around a bit until I'd had sex. I've never felt like doing it again, and Bill and I pretend it never happened.

But it changed everything.

I want to tell someone. I want to tell Jonah. Jonah is a year and a half older than me and he is my best friend. We have known each other since we were toddlers. He lost his family in the flood, too.

We used to see each other every day, tell each other everything, but we've both been dealing with our own stuff and we've sort of lost touch. Nana always asks after him.

'You used to live in each other's pockets.'

'You'd be so good for each other, the things you've gone through.'

'Don't you miss him?'

'I can't believe you don't miss him.'

She has been saying stuff like this for months.

I taught Sarah to float in the neighbour's dam. She caught on really fast, and in a really short time she was actually better at it than me. Mum said it meant I was a good teacher. But she was just being sweet. The truth was obvious; I hated the feeling of water in my ears, but it never bothered Sarah. This meant she could lie flat on her back, ramrod straight, her face almost immersed. We used to have competitions to see who could last the longest. She won every time.

It is exactly three weeks since the sex. The thought of it makes me sick.

I lay in bed last night, trying not to think about the events of the past year. But trying not to think about something just makes you think about it even more. In the end, I got up, threw a hoodie and trackies over my pyjamas, crept out of the boatshed and went for a walk.

I'm not afraid of the dark; I can thank Dad for that. Dad always said that the dark had its own brand of solitude, and that people who were afraid of the dark were often afraid of their own company.

'Relish it, Tom, it's the best time of the day and you have it all to yourself.'

So, I thought about Dad as I walked.

I ended up at Jonah's house. It was still the middle of the night, so I made myself comfortable on the front porch and waited for sunrise.

2

I guess Bill knew I couldn't stay at the boatshed, but when I told him, he packed all my stuff into his truck and drove me straight to Jonah's house.

'Bye, Tom,' he said. Bill's not much of a conversationalist.

'See ya,' I said. Then I cried. I'm not sure why.

Jonah's house is tiny. He lived here with his parents and a mangy cat called Runaway. His parents drowned, and they never found the cat. Jonah had fallen asleep on the lilo and no matter how high the water got, he just floated. Dead to the world.

After the flood, Jonah moved in with his grandfather. Jonah and Jonathan Whiting—Jonah is named after his grandfather—spent the next six months clearing debris, repairing and repainting. Jonathan hoped that the physical work would be therapeutic, that his grandson could work through his grief. But as soon as the house was liveable, Jonah begged to be allowed back home.

At first, his grandfather forbade it, saying sixteen was too young to be on his own. But Jonah was miserable. Living in town was noisy; he ached for the quiet, the acres of space. Most of all he missed his parents and the closest he could get to them was the house itself. So, the following March, ten months after the flood and with lots of conditions, his grandfather agreed. A month later, I moved in.

Jonathan hadn't counted on that.

Jonah's house is a half-hour walk from the Mavis Ornstein Home for the Elderly, which means I can visit Nana every day. I told her about moving in with Jonah. I didn't tell her why.

'Marvellous, darling,' she said on hearing the news. 'I never liked you living with Bill, but what could I do?'

'It's okay, Nana. It's all good now,' I said.

We chat as usual. Nana tells me she's starting an art appreciation class on Tuesday morning in the common room.

'Painting or drawing?' I ask.

'No, no, dear. Art *appreciation*,' she replies.

I'm not sure I know what to say, so I say nothing.

'A young woman from one of the city colleges is doing a study on *learning strengths in an ageing population,*' says Nana, in her officious voice. 'She popped in last week to meet us and she seemed very keen. Apparently we'll be discussing art in all its various forms.'

Nana abhors blandness on any level.

'I bet you'll be her favourite student,' I say.

Nana laughs and leans forward. 'Guinea pig more likely,' she says.

I stay with Nana until dusk.

Her evening meal arrives as I'm leaving. The smell makes me queasy.

Jonah's house has a bathroom with a separate shower and a small bathtub. We're on tank water so the bath doesn't get much use, but Jonah says I should treat myself every now and then. It's so good to be around him. I think he feels the same. It's like there's been no gap.

When I told Nana how easily we fitted back into our friendship, she said we had definitely passed the best-friend test.

'Really,' says Jonah, 'she said that?'

'Yep,' I answer.

Jonah and I are making dinner. I'm peeling things and he's cooking them.

'She said she has had a few friends over the years who didn't pass. She reckons that time apart is the key component to sorting the besties from the resties.'

'She said that?'

'No. She said "wheat from chaff".'

Jonah would love some chooks, but the flood took the sheds and most of the fencing. Bill has offered to help. Jonah said he would think about it.

Bill and I hang out occasionally. Jonah doesn't approve.

Last night Bill and I went night fishing at the inlet. 'If you've never been night fishing, you don't know what you're missing,' Bill says to Jonah, who just nods. Jonah finds it hard to speak to Bill because he knows about the sex. He also knows I have half Bill's baby inside me.

I grab my new tackle box and hand it to Bill (because it's heavy and I'm already carrying something of his).

'Jeez, Tom,' says Bill, as he feels the weight of my sinker collection.

'Is it as heavy as gold?' I ask him.

'Reckon,' he says.

The tackle box is from the FishMaster Super Series, and you won't believe it, but Mrs Peck gave it to me. I think Bill must have told her I was pregnant.

'There you go, Tom,' she said, her mouth all dry and clicking. As she handed it to me she suggested I look at all its features while she found Bill some line. It had been ages since Bill and I had been to Mingin's Hardware and Disposals. Mrs Peck looked desperate, but before she could drag Bill into the paint aisle, old Mrs Beakle came tottering in on her walker.

Mrs Peck rushed over to serve her. 'Oh, hello dear,' said Mrs Beakle, 'I'm just after a few mousetraps.' Mrs Peck went with her, shuffling along at Mrs Beakle's pace, '...and a couple of plate holders.'

Mrs Beakle took so long deciding between the free-standing or the wall-hanging plate holders that Bill decided to join them. 'Is that you, Bill dear?' Mrs Beakle asked when she noticed him. Bill quietly lifted the back of Mrs Peck's skirt. Mrs Peck dropped one of the mousetraps and lent down to pick it up. 'I think the free-standing should do the trick,' said Mrs Beakle, taking one down from the shelf. Then all three of them shuffled to the cash register.

By the time Mrs Peck had rung up the purchases, Bill looked ready to burst. Mrs Peck handed Mrs Beakle her change.

'Bye bye, dear,' said Mrs Beakle, forgetting all about Bill.

'Bye bye, Mrs Beakle,' said Mrs Peck's mouth, squashed onto the counter.

'I won't keep her out too late,' Bill says to Jonah as we leave the house. We walk through the dark to the inlet. Jonah waves to me from the window, me with half Bill's baby inside me and he my best friend.

It's funny, the fish you throw back. I'm sitting on the pier thinking about this when a little catfish, who looks a lot like the Sarah catfish, leaps straight out of the water. But before she splashes back in, she starts singing happy birthday and that's just like Sarah to remember. All the other fish at the inlet join in, until the splashing is so loud I can hardly hear the singing.

'Can you hear that?' Bill calls to me over the racket.

But I can't answer because I'm crying. I cry a lot these days.

Dad taught me to swim. Then he taught me to dive.

Diving can be scary if you don't learn early. Dad always said Mum was a case-in-point. Apparently she had tried to learn in her twenties and she never really got the hang of it, always preferring to jump in, feet first, no matter how much Dad disapproved. 'You're a bad influence, Angie,' he would shout from the bank. 'Don't watch, Tom.'

But I always watched. I thought she looked beautiful, swinging out over the dark water at the end of the rope, jumping in with hardly a splash. Mum and Dad took turns swimming and minding the kids, but Dad would always take me with him when it was Mum's turn to do the minding.

I loved it. He was a strong swimmer and could breast-stroke with me on his back, my arms around his neck. When I learned to hold my breath, we would play submarines, taking breaths on his count and plunging underwater. Mum never liked our games. She said we made her nervous.

I haven't been swimming anywhere but the pool since the flood. I fell in at Crabs Creek once, when Bill and I were fishing. I froze with fear. Bill had to haul me out.

'What is it?' I ask Bill when he hands me a small gift box. Bill has come to Jonah's house to visit me and the Minnow, who is half Bill's but is beginning to feel like half Jonah's. It's an odd feeling.

Even odder is Jonah's behaviour. Bill and he are being quite civil. I know the two of them had words the other night. Maybe they called a truce.

'Open it,' says Jonah. So I undo the ribbon and remove the lid. Inside is a tiny gold sinker on a chain. I place it in the palm of my hand and feel its weight.

'Oh, Bill,' is all I can say when I open my eyes.

'It's from Jonah, too,' says Bill.

Jonah grins at me. His face looks a bit awkward, and

I realise he has kept this secret for a while. 'Here,' he says, gesturing to me. Jonah has pianist's hands, long delicate fingers. He takes the necklace and clips it around my neck.

The boatshed didn't have a mirror but Jonah's house has three. I excuse myself and go to the bathroom. The bathroom mirror is smallish, but private, and I stand in front of it for a long time. Then I flush the toilet and go back out to the kitchen.

I am wearing the sinker the next time I go to Mingin's Hardware and Disposals.

'Well, what have you got there?' asks Mrs Peck, licking her lips and probably thinking how much better the sinker would look on her.

'I tell you what I've got,' I say, lowering my voice and leaning close to her ear, 'I've got half Bill's baby inside me and if you ever speak to me again I'll tell Mr Peck everything I know.'

In the quiet that follows, I watch Mrs Peck's mouth open and close. I notice little marks around her neck where she's gotten herself all tangled in someone's line. And that's not all.

'Here, let me get that for you, Mrs Peck,' I say, and I pull a shiny FishMaster Super Series hook out of her ugly bottom lip.

~

I haven't left the house for a few days. Jonah says I'm nesting. I doubt it. I've just been mooching around. Mooching and pottering. Mum used to say they were one-and-the-same, but I disagree. Pottering is when you actually do something, like pottering in the garden, whereas mooching is when you're thinking about it. I'm getting very good at both.

Jonah cooked fish and mashed potato for dinner tonight. I washed up and now we're sitting on the couch. Sometimes I wish we had a TV.

'You say something?' asks Jonah.

'I'm tired,' I say, 'I think I'll go to bed.'

I sleep in Jonah's room. He sleeps in his parents' room. I hear him crying some nights. We don't talk about it.

There's a loud knock on the door. 'We should make a run for it,' shouts the Minnow, jabbing me in the ribs. 'It's the *police*.'

I'm way too comfortable to move.

'I'll get it,' says Jonah. He gives my belly a gentle pat before he gets up to answer the door.

'Hello,' says a man's voice.

'Hello,' says Jonah.

The man introduces himself and his partner. They're detectives from West Wrestler. His partner is a woman.

There's a pause, then the woman asks, 'Are you Jonah Whiting?'

'Yes,' answers Jonah.

'Does a Holly Thomas live here?' she continues.

'She does.'

'Can we come in?' asks the man.

The Minnow has stopped swimming and whispers to me to be quiet. I wait for someone to speak. Jonah breaks the silence.

'Is something wrong?'

'We'd rather speak to Holly,' says the female voice.

'Well, she's asleep,' says Jonah.

The couch is old and soft with a really high back, so I'm invisible from the front door.

'Okay,' says the woman after a short pause, 'we'll come back another time.'

'Can I tell her what it is about?' asks Jonah.

'It has to do with Bill Hamperton,' says the man.

3

'I hate Mrs Peck,' I say, flopping onto Nana's bed. Nana is sitting in her armchair, reading or doing the crossword, I can't tell which.

'I'd rather you used an alternative to the hate word,' she says, throwing me her thesaurus.

I open it and choose a few that I like. 'Abhor, despise, detest, loathe. Be hostile to, have an aversion to, recoil from...'

'Tom! Stop being annoying and fetch me another snifter,' she says. 'And don't tell.' I sit up and feel around under her pillows until my hand finds the bottle.

I love Nana. I love Papa, too.

Jonah thinks it's strange that I love someone who died

before I was born. When I told him that I also loved the Minnow and that, strictly speaking, I hadn't met her yet, Jonah rolled his eyes.

'Well, Jonah, that's profound,' I said, letting him know that I clocked the eye-roll. It annoys me that someone as smart as Jonah can be so narrowly matter-of-fact sometimes.

'Profound?' he said.

I could tell he was irritated with the word, but I didn't care. I love it. I also love the word ravenous, but profound is up there as one of my favourites. So I let it hang. I'm much better than he is at taking the high ground.

'You know what I mean,' Jonah said, after a lengthy silence, 'it's *different*.'

Different. The extent of Jonah's argument.

'Of course it's *different*,' I replied, giving the word the same emphasis. 'But if I'm honest, Jonah, I'd have expected you, of all people, to understand.'

Anyway, where was I? Oh, that's right: Nana.

Nana is the best. She is wise and warm and totally adorable. Right now she's throwing back her fourth gin. Neat. Before lunch. Bill says she's pickled.

She used to smoke but she was told to stop, so she did. Just like that. 'If you had told me it would be that easy,' she had said to Dr Frank, 'I would have given up sooner. Nasty things. Don't you ever smoke, Tom.' No one's game enough to ask her to stop drinking.

'Some detectives came to see me,' says Nana.

I say nothing.

'Anything wrong, darling?'

'Nup.'

'You'd tell me, wouldn't you?'

I want to tell her that I miss the morning swims at the public pool and rock fishing at Crabs Gully and getting soaked-to-misery. But sometimes it's easier to lie.

'I'm fine, Nana,' I answer.

Nana knows I'm lying, but she trusts me. The thing is, everyone else seems to think I'm fragile, but Nana knows I'm tough.

'Tom, darling,' says Nana, interrupting my thoughts and handing me an empty vase, 'be a pet and fetch some ice.'

I walked down to the inlet by myself the other night. Jonah was asleep.

'Hi Bill,' I said.

'G'day Tom.'

'Anything biting?'

'Nothing much.'

We sat together, me with half his baby inside me and him with no one.

'Want some line?'

'I miss you, Bill.'

'Miss you too, champ.'

'I wish I had my FishMaster.'

'Who are you talking to?' It was Jonah, looking for me. 'I was worried.'

'I'm okay,' I said. 'I just miss stuff.'

Jonah doesn't fish. He can eat it, he just can't hook it. Says he feels awful when they look up at him. I know what he means, but if I said that to Bill he'd call me a sissy.

Jonah's not a sissy. He's just a gentle person who's not afraid to live with contradictions. I wanted to say 'antithesis' just then, but I couldn't work it in. Mavis (from Nana's home) says I have 'an inquiring mind that craves expansion' and gave me her thesaurus. The Minnow loves it. Her favourite word so far is 'cornucopia'. It's one of the words listed under 'profusion' (which is on the same page as 'profound').

I can't believe I haven't told you about the pet shop.

Fielder's Pets and Supplies. It's on the same street as the pool and the courthouse and right next door to the pub and it's the only pet shop in town. There used to be three, but the other two closed down after the flood. I think Mrs Blanket was the only one who had insurance.

'Hi, Mrs Blanket,' I say, letting the screen door bang behind me.

Mrs Blanket waves to me from the counter. 'Hi, Tom. Long time, no see.'

'Yep,' I say. I visit every week, sometimes more than once. But, I know what she means.

Mrs Blanket doesn't mention the Minnow.

After a minute or so, she goes back to whatever it was she was doing, leaving me to browse.

The bird cages are along the left wall, the fish tanks are along the right, and down the middle of the shop is an assortment of cages with rabbits and guinea pigs and mice. I walk slowly past the fish, letting the Minnow have a look, pausing every now and then to admire something special. But the best is at the back, and Mrs Blanket knows it: a mini-aquarium with a statue of liberty and four giant carp. Mrs Blanket almost lost them in the flood when the rising waters threatened to spill into their tank. From the mud on the pet shop walls, you can tell it got close. Everything else drowned or was washed away. I often wonder if the carp saw Sarah. She could have rounded the fire station, doubled back down Wesley Street, crossed over the park and come up through the lane and in the back door of the pet shop. I've asked the carp a few times, even described her in case she didn't give her name. But they're not speaking.

'They're getting even bigger, Mrs Blanket.'

'I reckon you're right, Tom,' she says, staring at them, beaming with pride.

'Which one's Oscar again?' I ask, not because I've forgotten; he's unforgettable.

'This is my darling Oscar,' she says and points to the most magnificent silvery-white fish whose enormous eyes are circled in blue.

'Look at that,' I whisper to the Minnow.

'I think he's dying,' she whispers back.

'What's the matter, Tom?' asks Mrs Blanket.

I'm fast asleep and dreaming about the police. They're at the front door, again, having another conversation with Jonah. Only this time they're sounding a bit irritated.

'Look, we really need you to bring her in,' says a voice.

'Otherwise, we could be forced to use force,' says another.

I hear the front door close. Open my eyes. Realise it wasn't a dream.

Jonah walks to my door, which is really his door, seeing as I'm sleeping in his room. 'You awake?'

I don't answer. I keep my breathing steady. The Minnow doesn't move a muscle.

'Okay, Tom, I'll buy it,' says Jonah, 'but they're getting insistent.'

'I know,' I say, out loud.

'Me too,' says the Minnow, just to me.

'Get up and I'll make you breakfast.'

'You hear that,' I say to the Minnow, 'he's making us breakfast.'

'Hungry?' calls Jonah as he walks the three steps to the tiny kitchen.

'Ravenous!' the Minnow and I call back in unison. The Minnow loves the word 'unison'. She says it describes us perfectly.

'Forced to use force,' I say halfway through my toast and eggs.

'Knew you were awake,' says Jonah, as he puts more bread under the grill. I pour us both a cup of tea.

'Jonah.'

'Yes, Tom.'

'Thanks.'

'For what?'

'For being my best friend. And for letting the Minnow and me move in.'

Papa had only just turned fifty when he died in a boating accident, almost thirty years ago. I overheard Nana telling Mavis that she thought it was ironic when Mum, Dad and Sarah also drowned. I'm not sure I agree with her choice of word. I looked up 'ironic' in the thesaurus and I don't like the alternatives any better. I prefer 'tragic'. Tragic has a much better list of alternatives, like 'ill-fated' and 'heartbreaking'.

Papa says I shouldn't worry. He says Nana was probably referring to the role water played in all of their deaths. Whatever. I still don't agree with her—especially as Papa told me he didn't actually drown. He got caught in the propeller. Apparently he was a real mess, and when Mum had to identify his body she decided to keep the truth to herself.

I can't be sure, but I think I saw Mum once. Bill and I were fishing at Crabs Gully and we kept seeing someone scuttling around the rocks. On our way home, Bill spotted a piece of fabric in one of the shallow pools, in the direction we had seen the person heading. Bill grabbed a stick and fished it out. When we got home we rinsed off the mud and laid it out in front of the pot belly. As it dried it filled the boatshed with the faintest smell of honeysuckle. Mum's smell. It wasn't a hanky, as we'd first thought, but one of the pockets from Mum's gardening apron. She must have left it for me to find, so I'd know she wasn't far. Papa says he hasn't seen her yet. Sometimes, he says, it takes time.

Most days, Papa hangs out at the Mavis Ornstein Home for the Elderly. He says he likes the company. Plus, everyone has one of his photos, so he feels like a bit of a legend.

~

The Minnow has a habit of prodding me awake. She is doing it now, and I'm trying my best to ignore her. The bigger I get, the more sleep I need, the more she prods. Right now, her fin is poking me in the ribs.

'Ow,' I groan, 'stop it.'

'There's someone at the door,' she whispers. 'It might be the police.'

'What should I do, Papa?'

'Well, you'll have to speak to them sooner or later,' he answers.

'Then I choose later,' I say, and roll over on my side. I try to fall back to sleep, but the disruption has ruined my chances.

'Ow, that one *really* hurt,' I complain, louder this time, following another sharp jab.

'I feel seasick on your left side,' she says, in her whiny voice. I roll onto my back and I listen to the quiet for a while. I decide it's safe to get up. The Minnow and I walk to the bathroom. I pee a lot. On the way to the kitchen I notice Jonah's bed is empty. It must be after nine. Jonah works at the pie shop on Saturday mornings. He used to work after school on Thursdays too. I'm not sure why he stopped.

The school was badly damaged in the flood. Classes were cancelled indefinitely and it seemed that they would never restart, until a politician turned up a week before Christmas, with a film crew. People were saying things like, 'it's a disgrace' and 'an appalling lack of essential services' and 'just a country town' and 'this would never happen in the city'. Two weeks later, trucks arrived. Building commenced on the first of January and halfway through January, four teachers appeared. The mayor put them up in caravans out the back of the town hall. Classes started in February, but had to be held in the hall for three months until the work was completed. The politician came back with the camera crew and opened the new school building on Mother's Day, in honour of the tragedy.

Jonah loves the new school. 'Better than the old building,' he says. 'All the rooms have air conditioning and there's a basketball hoop and they've fixed up the netball court and the toilets don't leak anymore and the boys have got a stainless-steel urinal that flushes automatically.'

'Anything else?' I ask.

'Lots of kids are missing.'

'Anything else?'

'Miss Pearson is there, but Mr Buckle drowned and Mrs Lee is too upset to return.'

'Is that what they said?'

'No, they said it was stress leave. She lost Ling and Betty.'

'What about "the fish"?'

'The new art teacher, Mr Wo, repainted.'

'What do you mean, repainted?'

'R.e.p.a.i.n.t.e.d,' he spelled out as though I was too stupid for tea cake. That's another Nana saying. Papa's favourite is 'too silly for roast beef'.

'But has he kept it like it was?'

I loved 'the fish'. Someone, years ago, had drawn an underwater scene across the western wall of the hall. I made a point of walking past it every day and knew every detail. The scene was a dark deepwater, and the fish and jellyfish were especially weird. No one really knew who the artist was. No signature, just 'the fish' written in the bottom right corner. But I'm guessing it was a bloke we knew called Dave McKewen, because it appeared around the same time that Mum started calling him 'a bit of a romantic'.

The entire thing was drawn in chalk.

Which was fine, while it never rained.

'You should see it, Tom.'

'I don't know,' I said. 'What if it's not the same? What if it's ruined?'

'Tom,' Jonah said, like he was trying to understand, 'it's beautiful. Mr Wo is really sensitive.'

'Sensitive?'

'That's what one of the other teachers said; that it was a sensitive rendition.'

I thought this over for a moment. 'I think I need to see it for myself,' I said.

'Well,' said Jonah, 'it's about time you came back to school.'

4

Jonah was right. I did need to go back to school.

I went the following weekend, but only to see Mr Wo's mural. Jonah and I walked there on Saturday afternoon, right after he finished work. He brought sausage rolls and sauce and we sat on the bench under the callistemon and ate them in silence, staring at the most beautiful painting I'd ever seen. The whole wall was covered in fish and coral and seahorses and jellyfish and seaweed, with tiny little starfish on the rocks and sharks in the background. And everything swayed with the current. It was even more beautiful than the original, although I wish that one wasn't lost. Now that I can never see it again, I'll probably imagine it differently. In years to come I'll be like Nana who remembers things the way she wants them to be and I'll lose Dave McKewen's drawing forever.

'Don't you like it?' asked Jonah.

'I love it,' I replied, and it was the truth.

'Then why the sad face?'

'When Mum lost her wedding ring, Dad saved up for two whole years and bought her a new one. It was beautiful. And Mum loved it. But I understand, now, why she cried when she put it on. It reminded her of how much she missed the old one.'

We sat there until it got cold. When we decided to leave, Jonah walked me the long way, past the new school buildings and the netball court. 'I know what you're trying to do, Jonah,' I said, 'but I'm not ready.'

'I know,' said Jonah, 'but you've already missed a year.'

It's a cold and windy Saturday. The Minnow and I have an hour or so until Jonah finishes work, so we're killing time at the pet shop. Mrs Blanket has the heating on, so it's nice and warm.

As usual I'm parked in front of the carp tank. And I'm daydreaming, which is why I get a bit of a shock when Oscar starts talking.

'I saw her,' he says. 'She had long brown hair and she was carrying a snorkel. I told her the snorkel was no good unless she was going to use it, but she said it was already too late.'

'Thanks, Oscar.' I can't believe he has finally decided to speak to me. 'Why didn't you say something earlier?'

'I was afraid I'd hurt you.'

'I'm tough.'

'I figured that out.'

If it is possible for a fish to smile, I'd swear he was smiling.

'The Minnow says you're dying.'

'She's a smart one, your Minnow.'

All four carp are side by side, almost motionless, looking at me and the Minnow. Mrs Blanket is fussing with a customer over a guinea pig.

'Oscar,' I say, pausing for a moment so this comes out right, 'why haven't you told the others?'

'There are carp and there are *carp*,' he replies. 'These three are sweet but uncommunicative. They'll find me floating on my side in a couple of weeks and the only one who'll grieve will be Mrs Blanket. This lot will just take it in their stride.'

'And me,' I say, 'I'll miss you heaps.'

'And you,' he says back.

I turn to walk out the door.

'Tom,' Oscar calls after me. 'The police were here asking questions.'

'Like what?'

'Just stuff about your family.'

'Thanks, Oscar.'

And then I think of something else. 'Did they mention Dad?'

'I don't remember.'

No one mentions Dad. I can't figure that out. Nana and Papa only talk about Mum. Of course, she was their daughter. But still. It's weird isn't it? Or maybe I'm just extra sensitive.

Dad was tall and thin and brown. He didn't like being inside and he spent all his time in the yard. He ate his dinner on the porch and he slept in the hammock. He didn't come inside to shower because he had a shower in the shed and a thunderbox behind the garage. Mum said he was a paradox. She could never figure out why showering in the shed was okay, but being in the house upset him. I really like the word 'paradox'. And I like all its alternative words except 'absurdity'. I don't understand how that one fits.

Everyone said Dad was talented. Mum said he could turn his hand to anything. We had a pond down the back. Dad had dug it close to the creek, with a little channel that fed it fresh water and a spillover to stop it flooding. In the middle was a fountain made entirely of scrap metal that he had scrounged from the Bunter and Davis recycling centre. Paul Bunter and Jacko Davis were Dad's mates and would give him anything he wanted. In return, Dad did all their electrics. Dad wasn't certified. He just knew how to do it on his own.

Dad and I got along better than Dad and Sarah. Probably because Sarah was a girly girl and I was a tomboy. And Dad never said much about anything and Sarah was a chatterbox. So Dad and I never argued, never got on each other's nerves, never got in each other's way. Mum said we swam in the same direction. I guess she was right about that. I never really thought about how comfortable I was around Dad until I had to fit in with Bill. Bill's a loner. People were surprised when he took me in.

I have a beautiful new dictionary. The Chambers English Dictionary. It has one thousand, seven hundred and ninety-two pages. I found this great word: 'solivagant'. It means 'wandering alone'. I was looking for a word to describe Dad, but I'm not sure solivagant is the one. But it's a great word.

Mavis bought me the dictionary for my birthday. She says her husband (who is really Papa) told her to buy it. Mavis says her husband is quite sure I'm brilliant. I know this is really Papa telling her these things because Mavis has a room-mate, Betsy Groot, and Betsy told me that Mavis has never been married. I suppose Nana has always known this, too.

'Thanks for the dictionary.'

'You're welcome, sport,' says Papa. He is sitting in the rocker on the front veranda. He looks out of place at the Mavis Ornstein Home for the Elderly. He looks too young.

'I know,' he says, when I tell him, 'but I'm old. I'll be eighty this November, just behind your grandmother.'

'You're not old, Papa. You're fifty.'

'No, Tom, I *was* fifty. Looks can be deceiving when you're dead.'

Sometimes Papa and I sit on the veranda all afternoon. Some of the old people say hi to him as they walk past, some don't. I guess some of them recognise him from his photo. Some don't see either one of us. Papa calls them the sad cases.

Every hour or so, he checks on Nana. They never chat or anything. Nana has imaginary conversations with him, rather than the real thing. But I think she knows. Little things give her away. For example, she never sits on the rocker if Papa is already there. She always walks around him, not through him (like the sad cases do). And it would be just like her to ignore Papa for thirty years as punishment for leaving her so young. Mum and Dad are lucky they are together. I wonder if they have found Sarah.

Sarah is three years younger than me. Well, in a way

she is four years younger now. It's a bit confusing. When she drowned she was three years younger and that is over a year ago. Anyway, in between Sarah and me, Mum had a miscarriage. Twins. I wish I knew if it was two boys, two girls, or one of each.

I often keep an eye out, just in case they're swimming around with the Sarah catfish. Jonah says I am getting ahead of myself when I worry about such things. He says to let it go.

I have never understood the let-it-go advice. What does it mean? Let what go? And how do you let something go if you're not even sure you're holding on to it? And anyway, what's so wrong with holding on?

Papa says 'letting go' is new-age bullshit.

I'm wandering back to Jonah's house in the dark, when I hear voices up ahead. The Minnow is fast asleep and I don't want to wake her, which is a shame because she's really good at hearing from a distance. The gravel is crunchy and noisy so I stand still. I recognise Jonah's voice. He is laughing about something. There is a man's voice. Older and more musical, almost like he's singing rather than speaking. I concentrate really hard but I can't make out any words.

'Tom!' It's Jonah. I don't answer. 'Tom!' he yells. 'Come and meet Mr Wo.'

I realise I am standing in a pool of light. The moon has appeared from behind a cloud and given me up. 'Okay,' I call back, trying to sound normal and not like a complete idiot, and I walk the thirty or so metres to the house.

Mr Wo is really young. His name is James and he says it's okay to call him that outside of school. He says he'd prefer everyone to call him James but that Mrs Haversham, one of the new senior teachers, thinks it is disrespectful. He has come to the house to meet me. This is Jonah's fault, I know it. He keeps avoiding my eyes.

'So, Tom, when do you think you'll be coming back to school?' Mr Wo says, getting straight to the point.

'I'm pregnant,' I say, and I can feel my eyes sting. Please don't cry in front of Mr Wo, I beg them, but they ignore me, and small tadpoles drop onto my cheeks.

'I'm so sorry,' says Mr Wo. 'Can I help?'

'It's all right,' says Jonah. 'She'll be okay in a minute, won't you Tom?'

I nod. Yes.

I stop crying, eventually. I blow my nose and look up to find Jonah and Mr Wo smiling at me. 'What?' I say to both of them.

'Nothing,' Mr Wo says. 'Are you okay to talk now?'

'I guess.'

'You haven't been to school since the flood, which means

you missed most of year nine and it's already September so year ten's going the same way.' He waits for me to speak, but I don't say a word.

'Okay,' he says, pausing to take a breath, 'how do you feel about using the next few months catching-up on year nine, with the idea of going into year ten next year?'

I look across at Jonah. 'It wouldn't be too bad,' he says.

He's right. But I'm still going to feel like a loser.

'Tom,' says Jonah, reading my expression, 'it's not like you're *repeating*.'

'Easy for you to say,' I reply.

'I know,' says Jonah.

The three of us are quiet for a minute or so. Eventually Mr Wo breaks the silence. 'So,' he says, 'I was thinking I could send some work home with Jonah. And I could come here once a week and check how you're doing.'

He raises an eyebrow at me. Jonah makes a face. 'How does that sound, Tom?'

'Good. It sounds good. Thanks, Mr Wo,' I say.

'James,' he says, and smiles. He's nice. He has a really pretty face.

Mr Wo—*James*—stands to leave. 'I'll see you Monday, Jonah,' he says. Then he turns to me and says, 'and I'll see you Friday afternoon, Tom.'

'Yes, okay,' I say, leaving out his name. 'Thanks.'

Jonah and I stand and watch him walk down the drive to his car.

'Oh, no,' I say to Jonah, 'I forgot to tell him how much I love the mural.'

'Tell him on Friday,' says Jonah.

5

The Minnow and I are down at the inlet. Jonah walked us there when he got home from school. He carried the Fish-Master. He's returning at dusk to walk me and the Minnow and the FishMaster back home.

I'm not really enjoying it. There is no Bill, there has been no sign of Sarah, the Minnow can't seem to get comfortable and, to put the pie in the freezer (another Nana saying), a cold breeze has picked up from behind Ponters Corner and I'm starting to shiver. I should walk home, but I don't want to leave the FishMaster.

'Look at who the cat dragged in.'

'Hi, Bill, I was just thinking that if you were here you could walk me home.'

'You're a lazy pike,' he says.

'I'm getting cold.'

'Come on then,' he says, helping me to my feet. 'Where's your line?'

'I didn't cast,' I say, feeling a bit silly. 'It's not the same,' I say, stopping before finishing the sentence. But Bill knows how the sentence ends.

He leans down and grabs the FishMaster. 'How's the Minnow?' he asks.

'Uncomfortable,' I answer.

It is Saturday afternoon and I'm in town. Jonah finishes work at two today, so I'm pottering around till then. The pet shop shuts anytime between midday and one-thirty (depending on business) so the Minnow and I go there first.

'You look well,' I say to Oscar.

'I've felt better, truth be known,' he says back. 'How's the Minnow?'

'Good, thanks. Can I ask you something?'

'Sure.'

'You know how the police have been asking around about stuff.'

'I told you they'd been here.'

'Should I go see Sergeant Griffin?'

I've known Sergeant Griffin all my life. He's been the

town cop for as long as anyone can remember. He, Dad, Paul, Jacko and Bill go way back. The five of them used to fish together, in the early days, before Dad met Mum.

Before the flood, Sergeant Griffin was everyone's friend. But the flood changed everything. Papa says it changed everyone, just some more than others.

But Sergeant Griffin looked on The Crossing as his responsibility, so he took it personally. Small communities can be like that.

Before the flood, things were predictable. Every Friday night, Sergeant Griffin would lock up the drunk'n'disorderlies. Bill says they weren't bad blokes if it weren't for the drink (although I'd have thought that was the point). Anyway, they would be given a bed in the cop shop, they would sleep it off and then, in the morning, the wives would come and take them home. Sergeant Griffin had been doing it for years. Some of the women thought he was better than a marriage counsellor.

The rain started to bucket down late Thursday, and by Friday evening the creeks had begun to rise. At ten o'clock, Sergeant Griffin did his rounds, collected a couple of drunks from the Pearl and Swine, tucked them in for the night and went home. But the rain turned angry around midnight. The storm became fierce. The power went out at one, and Sergeant Griffin was caught between staying at home with his wife and four-week-old baby daughter, or battling the weather and driving to the station. I don't know if he debated it much. From what I know of Sergeant Griffin, he has always been a cop first.

When the rain hadn't eased by two, he headed out. But he didn't get far. He had only driven a few kilometres when the flood waters threatened to sweep his truck into the creek. He had to turn back.

He made it home. The two men in the lockup drowned.

The flood peaked at around midday, Sunday. Mother's Day. When the water subsided, there were bodies and trees and mud and dead cows and upside-down cars and rubbish. It smelled pretty bad. Sergeant Griffin borrowed a tinny with an outboard and was rounding up people by first light, Monday morning. He rescued me from the roof of the fire station. I don't know how I got there. I don't know how long I'd been there. By the time he found me, I was cold and hungry and probably in shock.

Once I was safely in the tinny, Sergeant Griffin handed me a jar of peanut butter and a spoon. 'Here kid,' he said. 'Get that into ya.' I've never liked peanut butter, but Nana says hunger is the best ingredient in any dish. That's not really a saying; it's just an observation.

Sergeant Griffin spent all day Monday ferrying people

to the Mavis Ornstein Home for the Elderly, which was high and dry on the hill above town. It became a sort of emergency centre, and some of the residents had to be sedated because they couldn't cope with the intrusion. I was lucky. Nana showered me, dressed me in her flannel pyjamas, wrapped me in her arms and rocked me to sleep. For the next two weeks I ate, slept, cried and waited for Mum and Dad and Sarah to collect me and take me home.

Sergeant Griffin arrived one morning and told Nana that the house had been washed away. There was an emergency fund, he said, that would help with expenses. And the public pool was full of fish.

'You want to come along, Tom?' he asked. 'Help us get them out?'

Nana looked at me and nodded.

'Yes, thanks Sergeant Griffin, but I don't have any clothes.'

'It's fancy dress,' said Sergeant Griffin.

Nana said I could wear anything I wanted. She suggested her blue checked dress and Betsy Groot said I could borrow her fish brooch. But I'd never worn a dress in my life. So, instead, I wore Mr Greerman's grey-and-green striped pyjamas. Mr Greerman only ever wears pyjamas and he has an extensive collection. In fact, he has so many pairs of pyjamas that he houses them in a capacious wardrobe.

Okay, I made up the bit about the wardrobe. I just wanted to use the word 'capacious'. It's one of the alternatives for 'extensive' and Mr Wo (James) has been encouraging me to expand my repertoire. 'Repertoire' is listed in Nana's thesaurus under 'repertory'. My thesaurus leaps straight from 'repercussion' to 'repetition'.

Mrs Blanket is so devastated when Oscar dies, she closes the shop. Just for the day, not forever. The Minnow and I are standing outside, peering through the front window. But we can't see anything because of all the clutter in the middle isle. Under the 'closed' sign on the door, Mrs Blanket has written 'death in the family'.

'The Minnow knew he was dying,' I tell Jonah that night over dinner.

'Tom, you gotta be careful who you say that kind of stuff to,' says Jonah.

'What do you mean?'

Jonah is often like this. Mr Concerned. I tease him sometimes. 'So, Mr Concerned,' I say, 'what do you think about the situation in Afghanistan?' Jonah will usually start to smile. 'Really?' I say, pretending he has answered. Then I continue, 'So, Mr Concerned, do you have an opinion on the money crisis?' I keep on going until I've made him laugh.

'I'm serious,' says Jonah. 'You're not in the best situation.'

'Not in the best situation? Wow, Jonah, that's awesome.'

'I'm sorry, Tom,' Jonah says, because now I'm crying and we haven't finished dinner. 'I worry about you. What are you going to do when the Minnow arrives? Where are you going to live? What are you going to use for money?'

I can't listen anymore and I get up from the table and go to my room. Jonah's room. And I'm upset because he's right. I don't even have my own room.

'Tom,' Jonah says. He's standing outside my door—his door. 'Tom, can I come in?'

The weather's quite warm, which is lucky because none of my clothes fit. Jonah says I look beautiful. No one around here has ever shown off their belly before, and everyone has been quite lovely, touching it and putting their ear over my belly-button to listen to my little Minnow swimming around.

The police station is really a house. It is cream and white, with a half-porch out the front. You don't have to knock— even though there's a big brass knocker on the front door.

Mum used to say that if we were a bad town, there'd be more than one cop. She used to say Sergeant Griffin was proof enough. Nana always says 'the proof of the pudding is in the eating', but I'm not sure how that relates to Sergeant Griffin.

He looks up as I enter and smiles. 'Well, speak of the devil.'

'Hi, Sergeant Griffin,' I reply.

'We were just talking about you,' he says and he's nodding across to the couch. I turn and follow his eyes and there are two people, a man and a woman. I don't know them, which means I have no idea why they would be talking about me.

'These people are from West Wrestler,' he continues, 'and they want to ask you a few questions about Bill.'

'I haven't seen Bill in ages,' I say. My voice sounds shaky.

'There's something wrong,' whispers the Minnow.

'I know,' I say back.

'What's that?' asks the woman. But I don't answer. Something strange is happening. I think I should probably sit down.

'She doesn't look too good,' the woman says to the man.

'Something's wrong!' shouts the Minnow, and I know everyone can hear her because all three are staring at me.

'Quick,' says the woman, 'call an ambulance, her waters have broken.'

The Crossing is too small to have a hospital. Well, that's not exactly true; it has a hospital building, just no one in it. After the flood, only about half our population was left and we didn't qualify for funding. There's a sort of hospital at the Mavis Ornstein Home for the Elderly, but it can't do procedures. Nana had to have a procedure and they had to take her to the Mater Women's Hospital in West Wrestler. It's a really big town with two hospitals, one just for women. That's where they're taking me. The Minnow and I are in the police car. The police woman is driving. Fast. It's three hundred and twenty kilometres to West Wrestler and we're going to make it in less than ninety minutes. It would've taken too long to wait for an ambulance.

Jonah's grandfather, Jonathan Whiting, is Nana's best friend. He's younger than Nana and she calls him her spring chicken. She flaunts the friendship in front of Papa

Jonathan is a keen gardener and that's how their friendship started. He used to help Nana with the awkward stuff. She was very independent and got angry with him if he tried to do too much. She was famous for not speaking to him for two whole months after she came home from work to find he'd trimmed the hedge. It looked beautiful. All neat and square at the edges, with a gentle inward curve at the front gate. But the hedge had been Papa's job. Nana didn't really like the way it was going to the dogs, but that wasn't the point. The more unruly the hedge, the more everyone noticed that Jude Seth Wolkoff was dead.

The hedge had been testament to her loss.

'He was just being helpful.'

'He didn't know.'

'You can't blame him.'

'For god's sake, Valerie, forgive the poor man.'

It didn't matter what her friends said. She was too upset. She closed all the curtains at the front of the house so she wouldn't accidentally see the hedge in all its neatness. The neighbours didn't dare say anything because they rather liked Jonathan's handiwork. Most of them hadn't appreciated the hedge's deterioration. In fact, Nana told me that she'd overheard the next-door neighbours saying as much to a real-estate agent. They wanted to sell and move closer to their daughter, and they thought the state of Nana's hedge might threaten their sale. Apparently the agent had agreed, saying that the hedge had the potential to lower the tenor of the neighbourhood.

'What's a 'tenor'? I'd asked Nana.

'Don't interrupt,' she'd replied, 'I'm on a roll.'

Just like me, Jonah has only one living relative.

'Thanks for the vote of confidence,' says the Minnow.

'Can I get you anything?' the nurse asks me.

'I need my thesaurus and my dictionary,' I answer. 'Jonah

can bring them,' I add. Luckily, my waters didn't actually break. I have a weak membrane or something. Anyway, I've stopped leaking and I'm hooked up to a drip which is putting the water back in.

The Minnow has settled down for a nap.

'Dr Patek will be in to see you at about six,' says the nurse, as she leaves my room.

'She's a bit weird,' I say to Papa, who has been with me since this morning.

I have a phone next to my bed. It rings. 'That'll be Nana,' says Papa.

'Hello, Tom speaking.'

'Hello, darling,' says Nana. I wink across to Papa to let him know he is right. 'That lovely nurse put me straight through, said you have your own phone and everything.'

'And my own bathroom.'

'Oh, my,' she says to me. 'She has her own bathroom,' I hear her relay to someone. I hear Jonathan's gentle laugh.

'Hi, Jonathan,' I say via Nana.

Papa's face squelches.

'Hi, Holly.'

Nana has put her hand over the phone and she's saying something to Jonathan. She finishes whatever she's saying—probably admonishing Jonathan for calling me Holly—and clears her throat. There is a long silent pause. Nana and I never speak on the phone. Bill's boatshed didn't have a phone, and Jonah's house used to have one but it hasn't been reconnected.

'How's the Minnow?' Nana sounds relieved that she has thought of a question.

'She's sleeping,' I answer. 'They're putting in more water, so she'll be swimming around in no time,' I add. If Nana says something back we'll be having a conversation.

'The nurse who answered the phone. What's her name?'

'I'm not sure, Nana,' I say, 'but I can find out.'

Nana likes to know names. She'd like to get off the phone and show off to Jonathan and Mavis and Betsy Groot and say nurse Tamsin says this and nurse Tamsin says that. I don't know if the nurse's name is Tamsin, I'm just making that up.

'Well...' Nana says.

'Thanks for calling, Nana,' I say.

'Okay, dear.'

'Nana, can you ask Jonathan to ask Jonah to bring my thesaurus and dictionary?'

'All right dear, but remember you're a long way from The Crossing. I'm not sure how Jonah will get there.'

'But I *need* my thesaurus and dictionary,' I say, borrowing the Minnow's whiny voice.

'Okay, dear. I'll see what I can do.'

There is an enormous fish tank at the entrance to the maternity ward. If you take the lift, it's the first thing you see as the doors open. 'Thanks to all the staff, with gratitude and love, the Spencer family' says a small brass plaque. It has a sad tone to it. Like someone's missing.

The tank is home to numerous fish, about a hundred tiny snails with red and brown striped shells, some pretty awful plastic weed and one lone turtle. None of the fish are talking, which makes me think of something Oscar said. 'The tank's full of mixens,' says the little turtle.

'Mixens?' I say, hoping he will explain.

'Dunghill,' he answers. For a turtle, he is being extremely unhelpful.

'Shit,' he adds. I don't know if he is explaining or swearing. I wait to see if he's going to elaborate and, when he doesn't, I decide that he is what Papa would call a smart-arse. Papa says the best thing about smart-arses is they usually give themselves away pretty early.

'Uh huh,' I say, '...well, we were just passing.'

'Yeah, whatever,' he says.

I almost don't want to leave; he is such a complete tosser.

6

On Saturday morning, Mr Wo and Jonah drive all the way to West Wrestler to visit me and the Minnow. Jonah promised to bring my thesaurus and dictionary and Mr Wo is bringing me some schoolwork.

Jonah arrives first; Mr Wo has stopped at the cafeteria.

I wish Mr Wo hadn't asked me to call him James. Do I call him Mr Wo when he is visiting as my teacher? It's starting to do my head in.

I ask Jonah about it and he tells me he only refers to James as Mr Wo on school property. I smell something fishy.

'On school property?' I reply in a singsong voice.

'Don't be annoying, Tom.'

'Hi, Tom,' interrupts James Wo. *James Wo*: much better.

Neither of us heard him arrive. 'The doctor tells me you'll be here for a few weeks,' he says as he leans down and drops his bag on the floor.

'So,' he continues, pushing at the bag with his foot, 'I took the liberty of bringing some extra work.'

Jonah and I sit quietly. James Wo drinks his coffee. Jonah divides his time between staring out the window and staring at James Wo. Eventually James Wo pulls a chair next to my bed and talks me through each assignment. It takes about half an hour to explain everything.

He says that language is one of my strengths, so some of the tasks are aimed at broadening my skills. That, he says, will be the fun part. The rest is revision, plain and simple. He has designed a lesson plan to catch-me-up with the aim of entering year ten (with a baby in tow).

What did he say? The Minnow at high school? Is he high? I raise an eyebrow across to Jonah. He rolls his eyes back at me. 'You two finished?' asks James Wo, looking back and forth. Jonah's face turns red.

'Sorry,' I say. Jonah can't speak.

'Well, I think that's about it,' says James Wo, 'unless you have any questions.'

Yes, I'd like to know how my school's going to cope when I turn up with a baby. But instead I ask, 'Why does my thesaurus omit particular words?'

'Give me an example.'

'Repetoire,' I say, 'and there are others.'

James Wo smiles at me. I think he finds me amusing.

'I could compile a list.'

'You could, indeed,' says James Wo. He stands to leave. 'I'm going into town for a few hours,' he says to Jonah and me. 'Apparently West Wrestler has a fantastic library. I'll be back at about three o'clock. That should give the two of you time to catch up.'

He takes a small card from his pocket and tucks it into the side of one of the books that he's piled up on the table next to the bed. 'That's my mobile, if you need me. Otherwise, see you at three.' James Wo smiles, and he and his pretty face turn and leave.

It's quiet. Just me and Jonah. The Minnow has been asleep for what seems like days. I pat the bed.

'C'mon, Jonah, time to talk.'

Bill's truck is a twin-cab. He and I are up front and Paul Bunter and Jacko Davis are in the back. The four of us are driving up north to Minbayon Falls. Everyone goes there to fish for blue swimmer crabs, but the road is so bumpy that if I didn't have my seatbelt on tight, I'd have banged my head on the roof or the window, or both. As it is, I have one hand braced against the dash and I'm gripping the edge of the seat with the other. The drive to Minbayon Falls is never fun.

'You see that new fella in town, Tuesday?' yells Paul over the racket. I never bother talking to Bill while he's driving, mostly because he never bothers to answer me. But he'll answer Paul.

'Nup,' says Bill, 'but I heard he was sniffing around.'

Sniffing around. Bill's term for any unwelcome male and, as far as I can tell, they're always unwelcome according to Bill.

Paul leans forward, draping his arms over the seat between Bill and me. The first and second fingers of his left hand are stained a rusty yellow from years of roll-your-owns. 'Jacko's mate,' he says, hooking his right thumb back at the passenger sitting next to him (in case we'd somehow missed the fact that Jacko's riding in the twin-cab with us), 'from out west,' Paul continues, 'near Lake what's-its-name.'

Paul pauses a moment, but Jacko doesn't offer up the name of the lake. It's always like this. If Paul wasn't with us, the two-hour drive would go by in silence. But Paul's a talker. Bill says that Paul's the kind of bloke who sees a gap in the conversation and just has to fill it.

'You see him, Tom?' he asks me, when it is obvious that Bill has lost interest.

I shrug indifference and resume staring out the window. If I wanted, I could tell him that I saw a strange guy loitering around the pie shop. Saturday afternoon, while I was waiting for Jonah. Tall, red hair. Walked like he had ridden a horse all his life. Papa says a horse spoils a man. I'm not sure what that means.

Instead I say nothing. I like Paul. I've known him most of my life. It would be so easy to chat about the new guy; make guesses about what he's doing in town. But it would only make Bill edgy. Bill likes to be the one in the know. If I piped up, Bill would wonder why I hadn't told him first. Then he would question me about it; why I had kept it to myself. Stupid, really. Just a stranger standing outside the pie shop. But Bill can make a mountain out of any molehill, no matter how small.

'Jacko reckons he used to have family. The Fischers would be my guess, if his red hair is anything to go by.'

Shake Fischer. I think he was in the year below me. I didn't know him that well, but I'd chat to him every now and then. He had one blue eye and one brown eye. Apparently it ran in his family. That and the red hair. Shake was a nickname. I've no idea how he got it.

'You know the Fischers, Tom?' asks Paul, tapping my shoulder.

'I *knew* them,' I answer. 'Their house was in Keen Street, below the marker.' The flood sign in Keen Street had been incorrectly positioned at the high end of the road. No one had bothered to move it because, back then, it never rained. People thought it was funny.

'That's right,' says Paul, putting two and two together. 'Poor bastards.'

'Jesus, Bunter,' says Bill, 'could you get any more depressing?'

'Sorry, mate,' says Paul to Bill. Then the penny drops. 'Oh, shit, Tom...'

'It's okay,' I say. But there's a lump in my throat and suddenly I'm crying.

'Oh, Christ,' says Bill.

I turn my face to the passenger window and watch the view speed past. Paul starts to say something, but thinks better of it and instead gives my shoulder the briefest of squeezes before slumping back in his seat. A minute later, the cabin is filled with cigarette smoke. No one speaks for the rest of the trip.

Finally we turn onto Minbayon Falls Road. The gravel has recently been graded, promising a smooth, if dusty, ride. Bill tunes the radio and I fall asleep.

I'm in someone's house. It is beautifully furnished; everything looks like it belongs in a magazine. I am standing at the door to the lounge room and there is a woman, fast asleep, in bed. The bed is out of place among the sofas and lounge chairs.

I wonder if the woman is ill.

There are two other people in the room; an old woman and a young girl. The old woman is reading and the girl is playing with something on the floor. They ignore me. Maybe I'm invisible. I enter, close the door behind me, walk past the bed and across the room to the windows. Every step I take makes a squelching sound and when I look down at my feet I notice that the carpets are soaked. Water is seeping under the door.

The woman wakes up and gets out of bed. She is dressed in elegant trousers and a soft wool cardigan. She walks away from me, to a desk on the other side of the room. I stand there, with my back to the window, waiting for someone to notice me.

The sound of rushing water is deafening.

'Wake up, buddy.'

I'm vaguely aware of someone talking. I can hear the crashing roar of the falls, followed by a sudden blast of cold air on my face.

'C'mon, sleepyhead,' says Paul. I open my eyes to see him leaning against the door, lighting a cigarette. 'Jacko and Bill are over at the railing, waiting for us.'

I can't see them, but the noise and the mist tell me we've parked really close. I unclip my seatbelt and Paul helps me down from the cab.

'Sorry about before,' he says, as we walk across the car park. 'Sometimes I run off at the mouth without thinking. Next time, bloody kick me.'

'Don't worry about it,' I say.

Paul stops to grind his cigarette under his boot, then picks the butt off the ground and stashes it in his shirt pocket. Nana says it's an odd man who doesn't mind polluting his body, but is adamant about saving the environment.

'Piggyback?' I ask.

'Sure,' he answers and bends down to let me climb aboard.

Dad built Sarah and me a tree house in the magnolia. When the tree was flowering, the scent was almost overpowering. We had a rope ladder which was tied in three places to stop it swinging. I would have preferred it loose. What was the point of a rope ladder if it was fixed in three places? But Sarah got nervous if it swung around. Dad said that when she got older he'd untie the fastenings.

I decided that if the tree house had survived the flood, I'd fix it up for the Minnow. I could untie the ladder and teach her to climb like me.

'Would you come with me to the old place?' I ask Jonah. Jonah and I are lying side by side on the small hospital bed.

'You know your house got washed away.'

'I know. But it's over a year and I haven't been back. Not even to check on the tree house.'

'It's still there,' says Jonah. 'I went with James.'

'What do you mean, you went with James?' I can feel myself getting angry and I'm not sure why.

'Don't get upset, Tom. I should've told you, but I didn't think you cared about any of it.'

'Jonah Whiting. Are you insane? Of course I care. You of all people should know that.'

'I'm sorry,' he says.

We're interrupted by a knock on the door.

'Lover's quarrel?' says a nurse who has appeared in the doorway and is smiling at us approvingly. I have no idea how long she's been there. 'Stay put,' she instructs Jonah as he makes a move to get up, 'I'm just taking madam's pulse and temperature. Be out of your hair in two minutes, tops.'

Jonah and I turn slightly away from each other. I feel really uncomfortable and I know he does too. I wish he'd gotten off the bed while he had the chance. 'Okay, all done,' says Miss Efficiency. 'Lunch will be about ten minutes. You staying?' she asks, and looks enquiringly at Jonah.

'Yes,' I answer, as Jonah seems to have lost the power of speech. 'Jonah is staying till three.'

'Good,' she says, 'I'll ask the kitchen to add an extra

meal.' Jonah and I watch as the nurse writes something on the clipboard and hangs it back on the end of the bed. She looks at both of us and smiles as she leaves the room.

'Did you see that?' whispers the Minnow. 'She thinks you're a couple.'

'The Minnow's awake,' I say to Jonah, taking his hand and resting it on my belly. We sit like this for a few minutes. The Minnow obliges with a few summersaults. 'Jonah,' I say, 'do you think the police want to talk to me because they know the Minnow is half Bill's?'

'No,' answers Jonah. 'Bill has done something. The police have been questioning Paul Bunter and Jacko Davis.'

'Oh,' I say, lapsing back into silence. This is an unexpected turn of events. Maybe I'm off the hook. I'm about to ask Jonah how he knows what the police have been doing, when it dawns on me that he's acting weird.

'What's wrong?' I ask. 'You're not being yourself.'

Jonah shifts his body. He turns and looks at me, briefly, then refocuses on his feet. I realise I have no idea what's going on.

'Jonah, you're freaking me out.'

He clears his throat. I hold my tongue. He clears his throat for the second time.

'I've got a crush on James,' he says in a tiny voice. If we weren't sitting side by side, I would have missed it.

'A love crush?' I ask, taking his hand away from the Minnow so I can turn and face him. 'A love crush on James Wo?' My voice has come out high and squeaky.

'Just a crush, all right?' He folds his arms defensively.

'But he's a teacher,' I say, stating the obvious. 'He could lose his job.'

'Oh, sorry, Miss sleep-with-Bill-who's-old-enough-to-be-your-father.'

'Stop it,' I say, a bit too loudly.

'For god's sake, Tom, you've only just had your birthday,' meaning I was only fourteen when it happened, 'so don't you dare lecture me from your glasshouse.'

And then Jonah turns to look at me, letting me have the full force of the Jonah-Whiting stare. 'I haven't done anything wrong,' he continues. His eyes are glistening as though tears are close. 'It's just a crush.'

'But you took him to the tree house.'

7

After four and a half weeks at the Mater Women's Hospital in West Wrestler, the Minnow and I are allowed to go home. An orderly collects us and takes us to the ambulance in a wheelchair. I get a chance to check on the turtle while we wait for the lift.

I told Papa about him. Papa said he sounded rather unusual. He said that all the turtles he had ever met were fairly solid characters.

I notice that the tank faces the television in the nurses' station. God knows what he's been watching.

'Hi,' I say.

'Can you not tell when I'm sleeping?' he answers.

I add liar to the list.

'Papa says you're unusual,' I say, ignoring his rudeness, 'and he doesn't mean it in a good way.'

'Whatever,' says the little turtle, in a voice I recognise as lonely. He turns and slides off the rock into the water. I wish I hadn't said anything.

Eventually the lift dings, the doors open, and the orderly pushes me inside.

Once on the ground floor, after a brief pause at the front desk, we're wheeled to the ambulance bay. We pass Dr Patek talking to someone on her mobile. She makes elaborate hand signals to say she'll catch up with me in a minute.

The ambulance has a comfortable stretcher but I want to look at the view. As soon as she arrives, I ask Dr Patek if it's okay for me to sit up the front.

She checks with the driver.

'Not possible, I'm afraid,' she tells me. 'But there's a seat in the back if you'd rather not lie on the stretcher.'

'Damn,' whispers the Minnow.

The orderly manoeuvres me in to the ambulance.

'You take care of that baby,' says Dr Patek. 'I don't want to see either of you for another twelve weeks.' She smiles and waves as the driver reverses the ambulance out of the emergency bay.

'I like her the best,' says the Minnow.

'Me too,' I say back.

~

Home is Jonah's house. He said he regretted saying that stuff about me having nowhere to go. He said I can think of his house as my home for as long as I want. We've made plans to visit the tree house, although I'm not allowed to do anything strenuous for the rest of the pregnancy.

'Moderate exercise only,' Dr Patek had said, removing her glasses and giving me her serious face. 'How far is the letterbox?'

I looked at Jonah. 'About half a kilometre,' he answered. 'But it's a flat gravel road.'

'We'll see,' said Dr Patek. 'I'll check with Dr Frank each week and when he thinks you're strong enough, you can walk to the letterbox. In the interim, stay close to the house. And get the phone on. I've spoken to Social Services. They've been apprised of your situation. They can start with the phone. Call my office and speak to Pamela if you have any problems.'

I want to see Nana. The moderate exercise rule means that I can't walk to the Mavis Ornstein Home for the Elderly, so Jonathan Whiting collects me in his car. It seems every-one has been apprised of my situation. See the way I used 'apprised' just then? It's a James Wo initiative. Whenever I hear someone use an unfamiliar word, I should, first, write it down, second, look it up in the dictionary, third, familiarise myself with the word by writing it into at least three sentences and, fourth, practise using it in a conversation.

'Should I look it up in the thesaurus?'

'If you like, but only after you've completed all four steps. That way you'll have a more rounded comprehension of the word prior to seeking alternatives.'

I'm beginning to understand Jonah's crush.

Jonathan Whiting's car is an old Bentley, with cream duco and cream leather seats. Papa says it's a tribute to creaminess. Jonathan Whiting's favourite part of the car is the steering wheel. He tells me he had it custom made by the same people who make guitar plectrums. He said he asked for a shimmering mix of pearl, soft white and buttercup, and he is very pleased with the result. He runs his hands around the wheel while he tells me this, proudly admiring every facet. I hope he's watching the road.

'So, Tom, how long have you and Jonah been together?'

'Oh, we're not *together*,' I answer. 'Jonah's just letting me stay.'

'Well, he's obviously taking his responsibilities seriously, which is the main thing.'

'The Minnow isn't half Jonah's, if that's what you mean.'

Dad would've called that a conversation stopper. I prefer

looking out the window, so I'm happy that Jonathan Whiting is lost for words. My hand is resting on my tummy and I can feel the Minnow's tail-fin.

Nana has missed me.

'Let me look at you, darling,' she says, squashing my face between her hands. I've missed her too. Lucky I had Papa with me, but I don't tell her that. 'What did the doctor say?' she asks. 'Does he think you ought to rest more?'

'Dr Patek is a *she*,' I reply.

'Patek? What kind of name is that, dear?'

'Indian, I think. She's nice,' I say, 'and she's organised stuff for me at home.' But Nana is distracted.

'Jonathan,' she says, 'what kind of doctor is a patek?' Jonathan looks at me and smiles. I know that smile. It says welcome back. I feel so happy I could bust a gut. That's a Nana saying, but you probably guessed.

Nana has been knitting booties for the Minnow. She sent Jonathan to the wool shop, but (as it never gets very cold at The Crossing) he bought only one ball of wool in pale blue and eleven balls of cotton. Nana is knitting one bootie in each colour because she thinks matching pairs are boring. There is a line-up of completions on the card table.

I'm not sure why I'm quiet, so I don't know what to say when Nana asks. It's probably because I'm being swept along with the Minnow and I'm not sure I wanted any of this in the first place.

A counsellor talked to me at the hospital. She said all kinds of stuff about responsibility and preparation. I realised I'd only been thinking in small chunks. I told her I felt anxious whenever I thought about the future. The counsellor said it was an understandable reaction. She said this while staring at me and nodding her head which made me feel really uncomfortable. Papa, who was sitting beside me throughout the session, said, 'Just stare back at her until she looks away.' So I did. The counsellor flinched and looked down at her watch.

'Round one to you,' said Papa, elbowing me in the ribs.

Round two was all about the big picture. Bill always said the big picture was for Hollywood. 'Small chunks is all most folk can handle,' he'd say. 'Any more and you're just asking for trouble.' I realised I was starting to think of Bill in the past tense.

'The big picture is all about imagining the future,' said the counsellor, pausing and looking at me for a response.

'Oh, right, here we go,' sighed Papa, a little too loudly. I was glad only I could hear him.

I said nothing, so she continued. 'For example,' she said, 'I have a vegetable garden. At the moment I'm growing parsley and cauliflower, but I plan to add potatoes, beetroot and herbs. Maybe some spring onions.'

Papa couldn't help himself. 'What does she want? A round of applause?'

'You see,' she went on, mistaking my silence for interest, 'a garden is about planning and hard work, but I had to imagine it first, design it in my mind.'

'Oh, Christ, this is tedious,' said Papa.

I love Papa, but I hate it when he does this. He knows I can't react. If I tell him off in front of the counsellor, she'll think I'm crazy. But I had to say something soon—I just couldn't think of anything appropriate.

'Do you see?' she asked, one eyebrow raised.

'Yes, sport,' said Papa, standing behind the counsellor and leaning over her shoulder, smirking at me. 'Tell the nice well-meaning shrink that you see just fine.'

This was too much.

'No!' I said, almost shouting, 'I don't see.'

Papa fell silent and the counsellor leaned forward. She stretched her arm towards me and I thought she was going to touch my knee, but then she changed her mind and settled back in her chair. She waited for me to say something else.

'Before the flood, I used to think I'd be living at home with Mum and Dad and Sarah forever,' I said, 'or at least till I was old enough to leave school.'

'That's my girl,' said Papa. 'It's about time someone

stopped fart-arsing around and cut to the chase.' He was sitting next to me again. He took my hand and patted it gently. We both looked at the counsellor. She appeared distraught.

'I'm sorry for your loss,' she said. 'This must all seem so irrelevant.'

'No, really?' said Papa, in his sarcastic voice.

'Not really,' I lied.

The three of us sat in silence.

I could hear the hum of the fish tank down the hall.

'Don't worry, sport,' said Papa as we left the counsellor's room. 'No one is expected to predict the future.'

'Then why, when you're pregnant, does everyone assume there's some kind of plan?'

'A plan makes people feel comfortable, that's all.'

'Then why do I feel more comfortable without one?'

'I don't know, sport. You've always been something of a free spirit.'

Dad had great plans. Mum said so all the time.

'Papa,' I say, watching Nana through the window as she walks across the terrace and down to the pond. She's carrying a bag of stale bread to feed to the ducks and the magpies. 'When you die, do you feel responsible?'

Papa has a habit of scratching his ears when he is hiding

something. Nana says he could never keep a secret, because the scratching always gave him away. He is doing it now, and I can't for the life of me think why.

There is a commotion outside. I love the word 'commotion'. I have a notebook that I carry with me everywhere. I try to write a new word in it everyday. Commotion was Thursday's word. Anyway, it seems Nana has caused the commotion by falling into the pond. Papa and I stay put. We both know she dived in. We have seen her do it more than once. There are nurses and orderlies running about and making a fuss. Nana will be lapping it up.

'Hi, Tom,' says Sergeant Griffin, startling me. He is alone. 'Can we talk for a minute?' he says, moving over towards the chair occupied by Papa.

I used to feel dreadful when this happened. Sometimes I'd leap to my feet and offer my seat, or I'd say I felt like going outside; anything to avoid upsetting Papa. But we both know the score. So I watch and wait. At the last minute Papa moves and Sergeant Griffin sits down.

'Your grandfather is quite the star around here,' he says, nodding at the framed photo on the wall.

'Yeah,' I say, 'Nana gets special deals on print runs over a hundred.'

This is an in-house joke. Mike Spice started it after Nana refused his dinner invitation. It must have been hard for him, especially when one of Papa's photos turned up in his room.

'Last time we saw each other,' Sergeant Griffin continues, 'you were coming into the station. I just wondered what it was you wanted to talk about?'

Bill always said Griffin was careful and considerate. And ultra smart.

'I forget,' I say. 'So much has happened.'

'Yes', he says with a nod. 'You'll remember there were two people from West Wrestler,' he pauses. 'Detectives,' he says, pauses again, catches my eye. 'Well, they were asking about you; they wanted some information about Bill.'

'Uh huh.' My heart has started to race. I can feel small beads of perspiration on my upper lip. 'I've been in hospital, Sergeant Griffin,' I say. 'I don't know why the police would want to speak to me.'

'Of course not,' he says sweetly. 'They are just running their enquiries, is all. I said I would follow up on the loose ends. You're just a loose end, Tom. Nothing to worry about.'

But I am worried. I have a growing feeling of dread in the pit of my stomach. The Minnow can feel it too.

'Well, if it isn't Miles Griffin!' says Nana, appearing in the doorway. Her hair is plastered to her head and she has a towel wrapped around her shoulders. 'You're a sight for sore eyes, young man,' she says. 'What brings you out here?'

Sometimes Nana's timing is impeccable. That will be today's word.

Nana and Sergeant Griffin start up a conversation, so I excuse myself and leave the room. Papa has disappeared. He is probably down at the car park, checking out Jonathan Whiting's car—which is good because I want some time alone. I need to sort through some of my feelings about Bill before Sergeant Griffin springs another visit. I sneak quietly along the front veranda and around the corner. I'm heading for the day bed at the far end. I can see it's unoccupied, but I have yet to get past the common room without being seen. This isn't easy because there are windows running the full length of the veranda. If it weren't for the Minnow, I would crawl some of the way, but she makes that impossible.

'G'day, Tom,' says Hazel, leaning out of the doorway.

Hazel is the residential unit manager. She ran the hospital wing for almost a decade before she was transferred. Nana adores her.

'You after some peace and quiet, darl?' she asks.

'Heading for the day bed, Haze, but I was hoping to get there unnoticed.'

'Common room's deserted,' she says, with a wink. 'Your granny's latest pond-dive was too much excitement and everyone, except Campbell, is off having a nap.' Campbell is the common-room cat.

Hazel walks over to me, takes my arm and leads me to the day bed. She helps me up, arranges the pillows under my knees and covers me with one of Betsy Groot's hand-knitted blankets. 'There you are, ma'am,' she smiles. 'Will there be anything else?'

'Thanks, Haze,' I say. 'You're the best.'

'Give me a yell when you want to get down. Campbell and I will be in the office, catching up on paperwork.'

8

Bill has secrets. I know this because I've seen them: small canvas satchels stashed in various cubbyholes in and around the boatshed. He used to move them from one spot to another every few months, usually late at night when he thought I was asleep. But how could I sleep? I was homesick. I missed Mum's laugh and Sarah's morning snuggles. Mostly I missed the sound of Dad rummaging around in the dark.

The first time I heard Bill digging, I thought it was Dad. I snuck out of bed to get a better look and there he was, spade in hand, like always. I sat on the floor and watched him, filled with relief that the nightmare was over and my life was back to normal, until something made me realise that I was watching Bill. Suddenly I felt sick and frightened. I watched for hours, frozen to the spot, as Bill dug a hole large enough for me. It was still dark when he finished and I crawled back into bed. I lay awake till dawn. I was living with a stranger who, by the look of it, was going to kill me and bury me in the yard.

In the morning the hole was gone and the ground was flat. I walked over the spot a few times, trying to feel if it was looser than the surrounding dirt, but it all felt the same. 'You worried about something, buddy?' asked Bill, leaning against the screen door. I realised I had no idea how long he had been watching me.

Bill cleared his throat and spat the contents onto the dirt.

'Because you look like you're pacing,' he said.

Mrs Blanket's assistant, Clare, is from Kansas. I know Kansas from *The Wizard of Oz*. Clare moved to Australia to be a teacher but changed her mind once she arrived. She decided she liked animals more than kids, and she worked as a jillaroo for a few years out west, until the drought forced her to look for work in town. It flooded not long after she settled here. She says if she was ever going to leave, she would have done it then. I'm glad she stayed.

'You're looking a bit tired,' says Clare, using her index finger in a simple back and forth motion to mimic the dark circles under my eyes. 'You need a sleeping tonic,' she says, and disappears out the back.

'Hi, Mrs Blanket,' I say, waiting for Clare.

'Hi, Tom,' she says. 'You're looking tired.'

'Sorted,' Clare says, reappearing suddenly, clutching a small glass jar and a large syringe.

'You ever had a Kansas sleeping tonic?' she asks, knowing my answer. I shake my head, no. Clare walks over to the axolotl tank and hands me the jar. With the syringe she draws a full measure of water. 'Well,' she says, looking at the jar in my hand. 'Open it.' I take off the lid and she squirts the water in. She does this twice more until the jar is about a third full. 'Follow me,' she orders, and I follow her back to the counter. 'Give it here,' she says, reaching for the jar. I hand her the jar. 'And the lid,' she says. I hand her the lid.

'Now, Tom,' she says, in what I imagine is her teacher's voice, 'this is important. Do not drink this. If you do, you'll sleep for a week.' I'm not sure if she's joking or serious. She screws on the lid and places the jar in front of me. She rests her forefinger on top. 'At night,' she continues, 'just before you get into bed, remove the lid and place the jar where the moonlight can reach it.'

'What if it's cloudy?'

'When there's no moon, it won't work.'

'That's all I do?'

'No,' she leans closer, 'you need to stir it.' Clare reaches under the counter and rummages around for a bit. 'I don't seem to have what I'm looking for,' she says, more to herself than me. 'Wait a minute.' Clare walks through the shop and disappears outside.

'She's a strange one,' says Mrs Blanket, 'but her cures seem to work. She gave old Mr Cravensbourne a heart tonic from the carp tank a few weeks ago. He swears he's never felt better.'

I look at the carp. Three blank pairs of eyes look back at me. 'Was that around the time Oscar died, Mrs Blanket?' I ask, then wish I hadn't.

'Here you go,' says Clare, walking back through the shop with a twig in her hand. 'Stir it with this, slowly and carefully.'

'For how long?'

'Good question. Five turns should do it. Maybe six. You'll sleep like a baby.'

'Jonah,' I say, calling out to the front porch from the bedroom, 'do you think you can walk me down to the inlet?' Dr Patek has spoken to Dr Frank and they both agree that the moderate exercise rule can be extended to include the inlet as well as the letterbox. I can't see the point of walking to the letterbox. 'Jonah,' I call, louder this time.

Jonah Whiting is a dreamer. It's one of my favourite things about him, although it can be annoying when I want an answer.

'What?'

'That took a while,' I say. Papa calls it answering via satellite.

'Yeah, well, I was thinking.'

I walk out to the porch with the FishMaster. Jonah's still eating his breakfast. He's sharing his toast with a baby magpie, and he has the little bird eating out of his hand.

'Jonah,' I say, 'if the FishMaster had wheels I could walk to the inlet on my own.' I had been thinking of borrowing Nana's shopping trolley. Actually, it was Papa who suggested it. He said Nana doesn't use the trolley anymore because she gets Jonathan to carry all her shopping. Papa nicknamed Jonathan Whiting 'the bag man'.

'It's okay, Tom, I don't mind carrying it.'

Jonah says that, but sometimes I wonder.

'But,' he says, turning to face me, 'I could hook it up to my old skateboard if you're serious about walking on your own.'

'Now?'

'No, not now. Later.'

'Let's go then,' I say. 'Just give me two secs.'

I used to be able to fish on an empty stomach, but now I need supplies. I pack some bread and fruit into an old lunchbox, fill a bottle with water and, remembering how uncomfortable the pier has become, grab a cushion off the couch.

The walk to the inlet is uncomfortably quiet. Jonah seems a million miles away, too far for me to reach. So I get a fright when he speaks.

'You remember Caleb Loeb?'

'Jeez, Jonah. I almost dropped the Minnow.'

'Funny.'

'Caleb Loeb. Tall, skinny guy. Pretended to have a bit of a thing for Mrs Lee.'

'That wasn't pretend. He was just young. You're so wrong about people, Tom.'

'Is that right? Was I wrong about you?' My trump card.

'Yeah, okay, you've always been right about me. But you're wrong about Caleb.'

'Go on then, enlighten me.' Enlighten. It means lots of things, some of them religious, but right now it means I want information.

'I think I'm in love with him.'

'What happened to the crush on James Wo?'

'Still a hundred per cent. But Caleb is my age and, well, he understands what I'm going through.'

'You're sure about that?'

'I told him.'

'You told him you're gay or you told him about the crush on James Wo?'

'Both.'

'Oh, Jonah. What have you done?'

Caleb Loeb is a piece of work. He has always been a bully, but not overtly, more in an underhanded way. Papa taught me about overt and covert, so don't go thinking I've only known about them since I met James Wo. Anyway, Mrs Lee is a perfect example. Caleb Loeb carried on all through year six, batting his eyes at her, carrying her things from the car to the classroom, cleaning the whiteboard. If any of the boys tried to tease him about it, he would walk up to them and dare them to repeat what they had said. One kid, Jai Graython, called him 'teacher's pet' to his face, and Caleb Loeb broke his nose. When he was asked why he did it, Caleb burst into tears and said it was a mistake and that he never meant to do it. Mrs Lee spoke to Jai's parents and Jai had to apologise to Caleb in front of the class.

The thing is, Caleb Loeb despised Mrs Lee. I knew this because Papa taught me how to read the signs.

Every Wednesday is poker day at the Mavis Ornstein Home for the Elderly, and Papa, who jokes that poker is one of life's great games, likes to walk around the room, surveying the players' cards and making comments. That's how he taught me about the 'tell'.

Papa would look at a player's hand (and I may as well tell you that he often chose Mike Spice), and it was my job to figure out whether the hand was good or bad. Papa would give me hints. For example, he would point out what Mike was doing with his face. Papa said that Mike Spice was green, meaning he hadn't played much poker, so he was a good subject because he was still figuring out how to mask his feelings. The trick, Papa said, was learning what to dismiss and what to watch. A practised poker player, like Nana, was almost impossible to read.

I learned that just a flicker of an expression could betray the truth. That is how I knew Caleb Loeb's crush on Mrs Lee was an act. But what he was doing now was much, much worse. He had convinced Jonah that he was his friend, his confidant. And Jonah was falling for it, hook, line and sinker.

I wanted to kill Caleb Loeb.

At the inlet, I get myself settled and wait for Jonah to leave. Since the police turned up, Bill won't appear unless I'm alone.

'Okay, then,' says Jonah. I say nothing. 'I'll be back later,' he says, needlessly. Then he walks away without looking back to wave. Bloody Caleb Loeb.

'Seen Sarah?' Bill asks, sneaking up on me.

'Shit, Bill, you scared me half to death.'

'Swearing doesn't suit you.'

'And parenting isn't your forte.'

'Forte? You using one of Wo's words?'

'Don't be an arsehole, Bill.'

We're interrupted by a loud splash. Both of us turn towards the source of the noise, but there's barely a ripple. I turn back to Bill, but he's gone. Well, I think to myself, if you can't take the heat.

I open the FishMaster and take out the fishing line that I prepared at home. I've wound it around an old toilet roll so it won't get tangled.

'Why'd you bother bringing the FishMaster?' It's Bill. He's back.

'Why do you bother speaking?' Nana says if you can't say something nice, don't say anything at all.

'That a Nana saying?' Bill always knows what I'm thinking.

'Get out of my head, Bill,' I say. 'My thoughts are my own private business.'

Bill sits down on the jetty and hangs his legs over the edge. 'Water's low,' he says, stating the obvious. He reaches into his fishing bag and pulls out a roll of line, takes a hook from his shirt pocket and turns to me. 'You want to hand me one of your fancy sinkers?' he asks, looking at me coldly and challenging me to refuse.

'Sure, Bill.'

I'm not going to take the bait. I know his moods, and this one is always ugly.

I hand Bill the Townley-Morris fiske sinker. I made that name up, if you're wondering. All my sinkers have names. Most of them come packaged with brand and model names, although sometimes the model is just a number. I rename sinkers if I don't like the sound of the brand, and I *always* name the sinkers I find. It's surprising how many get washed up, caught in old bits of line. Sometimes I find them on the pier. Once I found eighteen sinkers in an old tin. I keep those in a separate compartment in the FishMaster, just in case one day I meet their owner. Anyway, the Townley-Morris had a TM printed on it, so I named it to fit the initials. It got the 'fiske' because I found the sinker at Fiske Point.

Fiske Point is a small bay with a sand spit that extends out from one side and dense scrub on the other. We usually fish from one of the bay's feeder creeks, but you can also fish from the beach and from the sand spit. The sand spit is pretty amazing. At low tide it stretches for about two hundred metres and you can walk all the way to the point. The sand, which is only a few metres wide, is all there is between the clear calm water of the bay on one side and the deep choppy ocean on the other. The only downside is that the ocean breeze kicks sand into your eyes almost continuously.

One of Fiske Point's bigger creeks—Bill and I named it the Rumbly, I forget why—is wide enough for the tinny. You have to row hard against the current for about three hundred metres until it opens out into a large lake. The water's deep and dark and the fishing is good. If it wasn't so hard to reach, we would probably fish there more often. One time, we left the tinny tied to the embankment, but walking through the scrub was even harder than rowing, so we never did that again. Anyway, I was telling you how I found the sinker. It was late one afternoon and Bill and I were fishing at the Rumbly's lake. It was surprisingly quiet—not much was biting. The last of the sun was flickering through the trees, and as it landed on the branch of an oleander tree, something shone out towards me like a torch. Bill was asleep so I pulled up our lines and steered the tinny over to check it out. The rest was easy. The branch grew out over the water and was low enough for me to reach. I felt around for the source of the shiny thing and found the sinker. Luckily Bill was dead to the world and didn't stir even when the breeze picked up and leaves rained down on him. The sinker was attached to a piece of line that was wound around the branch. Unwinding it took a while. But by the time Bill woke, we were back in our spot, lines recast.

'How'd the boat get full of leaves?' Bill said as he checked his line.

'Well, you should know,' I answered. 'Seeing as you say you never fall asleep.'

'Touché,' said Papa.

9

Bill attached the Townley-Morris fiske and cast his line. I watched him out of the corner of my eye. I've learned to keep watch when Bill is in one of his moods. I was kind of wishing Jonah hadn't left, so I was relieved when Papa appeared. Papa doesn't like leaving the Mavis Ornstein Home for the Elderly, but he has started making it a bit of a habit ever since the police showed up. I haven't had the nerve to ask Bill what they want with him.

If you're wondering why I named the sinker the 'fiske' and not the 'rumbly', it's because I'm saving the name Rumbly for when I get a pet. When I was little I really wanted a cat, but Dad forbade it. He said they were vicious killing machines. We used to have a feral cat problem at

The Crossing before Dad sorted it. Dad was always awake at night, so killing cats gave him something to do. Nana referred to it as *T-triple-C* (The Crossing's Cat Culling). She said our town was indebted to Dad's insomnia.

Mrs Blanket doesn't keep puppies or kittens and she only sells male rabbits and guinea pigs to prevent uncontrolled breeding. 'You can't trust most folks with pets,' she says. 'They're either too lazy or too broke to have their pets neutered, or they let them go feral when they're bored with them and we end up in all kinds of trouble.' She stopped selling carp when she heard about people letting them go in creeks and she absolutely refuses to sell pets in December because she disagrees with pets as Christmas presents.

I think Rumbly would make a great name for a turtle.

When I woke up, Mum was smiling at me. She looked just exactly the same.

'Mum,' I said, but no words came out. She reached over and touched my cheek with the back of her hand. It felt wonderfully familiar.

'Don't speak, pet,' she said, 'the doctor will be in to check on you soon.'

I tried to swallow but it hurt. I tried to feel for the Minnow but my body seemed wooden and distant. It was hard to keep my eyes open, so I let them close.

'She opened her eyes,' I heard Mum say.

'Good, very good,' I heard someone reply.

'It's a good sign, then?' Mum asked.

'Better than good,' the same person answered.

I could hear small beeping sounds. Someone lifted my arm and held my wrist. The same someone was taking my pulse. I wondered if I was back at the Mater Women's Hospital in West Wrestler. I tried to open my eyes to check, but my eye lids were too heavy. 'Mum,' I said again.

'I think she's trying to speak,' Mum said in her worried voice.

'That's what it looks like,' the wrist holder answered, 'but it's probably just a gagging reflex caused by the tube in her throat.'

'But what if she's trying to speak?'

'The tube will make it impossible.'

Mum brushed my cheek with her hand again, slowly this time.

'Try not to speak, puppy. The doctor won't be long.'

Nothing's biting. The inlet is conveniently close to Jonah's house, I just wish it was a more reliable fishing spot. I had planned to catch dinner, but it looks like we'll be eating something out of a can.

'Watch out!' shouts the Minnow. I turn towards Bill.

'What?' he says, looking at me accusingly.

'Nothing,' I reply.

'Watch out for what?' I whisper to the Minnow.

'Over Bill's shoulder,' she answers.

I turn to look. There is nothing there. She's scaring me.

'Something's about to happen,' she says. 'Trust me.'

Once, when I was four, I lived outside with Dad for almost a month. I loved it. I slept in the hammock, ate strange things that he cooked on the fire, spent each day with him doing whatever it was he was doing. One morning, at Bunter and Davis, while Dad was hunting for roofing iron, I found a box of wooden pegs. They were large and old and someone had made them into toy people. Each peg had clothes and a painted face, and hair made out of yellow knitting wool. The three pegs wearing trousers had yellow wool moustaches and the four pegs wearing dresses had rosy red cheeks and big red lips. I decided all seven were girls.

When I showed my discovery to Paul Bunter he said I could keep them on one condition; that I moved back into the house with my mother. I remember feeling so torn. I loved being outside with Dad. I loved sleeping in the hammock and rummaging around at the scrap yard.

I looked up at Dad, and he just smiled his Dad smile.

'Mum misses tucking you in,' he said.

'I know,' I said, because I missed her tucking me in, more than I'd realised until that moment. So I moved back into the house with my new toys.

Two men stood at the entrance to the jetty. Both were holding rifles. Bill was facing me so I wasn't sure if he knew.

'We might have to swim for it,' suggested the Minnow. She was serious.

'Bill,' I managed.

'One or two?' he asked.

'Two,' I replied.

'They moving?'

'Not yet.'

'How far?'

'Jetty entrance.'

'He's going to bolt,' said Papa.

'What's going on, Bill?'

'Too hard to explain,' he answered. 'Just tell me if they do anything.'

'One of them is talking on the phone.'

'What's the other one doing?'

'Nothing. Bill, they've got guns.'

'Shit.'

Great, I thought. I should have walked to the letterbox.

'Whatever happens, Tom, stay perfectly still,' said Bill.

'They've no interest in you, so don't give them any reason.'

'What are you going to do?'

'I have no idea,' he said, but as the words left his mouth he folded forward and toppled into the water.

'Bill!'

'Don't move, Tom,' said Papa.

One of the men ran towards us and the other took off in the opposite direction.

'I didn't even hear the bullet,' I said to Papa as I realised what had just happened.

'There was no bullet,' said Papa. 'I told you he'd do a runner. Sneaky bastard is probably under the jetty catching his breath.'

I wanted to lean down and have a look.

'Hey kid, you see where he went?' The man had a handsome face. He wasn't even panting.

'Yes, straight off the edge. I thought you shot him.'

The man with the handsome face lifted the rifle over his head and placed it carefully on the jetty, crouching down beside it. He leant forward and scanned the dark water of the inlet. 'How deep is it?'

'Not sure, I've never been in.'

He flattened his body against the deck and pulled his torso far enough over the edge to get a look underneath. Papa nudged my arm.

'Look towards Ponters Corner,' he whispered. 'Left of the split rock.'

Directly opposite, on the inlet's farthest bank, was Bill. I have no idea how he made the distance without being seen. He was sitting perfectly still, tucked in behind some lantana. I would never have seen him without Papa's help.

He was watching us. No, he was watching Mr Handsome.

'Tom!' shouted Jonah.

I got such a fright, I screamed. Mr Handsome jumped to his feet and grabbed his rifle.

'It's Jonah and James Wo,' I said, trying to calm myself.

Papa and Mr Handsome and I watched Jonah and James Wo walk up the pier towards us.

'What's going on?' Jonah asked. 'Who is this?'

I looked across the inlet. Bill was gone.

Nana wants to know everything. Mavis Leitch and Betsy Groot and Mike Spice have crammed into her room and the four of them are buzzing with excitement. Nothing much happens at the Mavis Ornstein Home for the Elderly, so the news of my lucky escape from Bill and the two men has spread like wildfire. Jonah and James Wo have been allocated hero status, and Hazel has invited them for Saturday lunch in the common room.

Nana's room feels rather crowded.

'I'm off,' says Papa as Jonathan Whiting appears in the doorway.

'Hi, Jonathan,' everyone says in unison.

'I see you're already here, Miss,' Jonathan says to me.

'Sergeant Griffin drove me,' I say.

'Oooh,' says the pack.

'Here, Jono,' says Nana, patting the seat next to her on the couch. 'That grandson of yours is such a darling.'

Jonathan Whiting beams with pride and takes his place next to Nana. 'Tom was just telling us how the man flattened himself on the jetty. Go on darling,' instructs Nana, as five elderly sets of eyes turn to face me. 'We're all dying to hear what happened next.'

I told them everything except the bit about seeing Bill hiding behind the rock. Sergeant Griffin said it was best to keep that between him and me.

After Jonah and James Wo collected me from the inlet (which was fairly uneventful: Mr Handsome just excused himself and left), Jonah called his grandfather and he called Sergeant Griffin.

Sergeant Griffin drove me and the Minnow to the station. Sergeant Griffin then phoned one of the visiting detectives who told him to take my statement. Sergeant Griffin types very slowly so this last bit took a while.

The next morning, Sergeant Griffin was back. Jonah woke me.

'There's someone arriving this morning from head office in West Wrestler,' Sergeant Griffin said to me over Jonah's shoulder. 'She'll be here in about thirty minutes. She wants to make an identikit of that man who was after Bill.' This was a big deal for a small-town cop and you could tell he wanted everything to run smoothly.

I had a shower and got dressed and ate breakfast. Then Sergeant Griffin took me and the Minnow back to the station.

The police sketch artist was really nice. She had beautiful long fingers and a pointy nose, and she had a habit of resting her pencil against her cheek while she looked at me. Together we drew Mr Handsome. Then Sergeant Griffin drove me to the Mavis Ornstein Home for the Elderly to see Nana.

'Thank you for your help, Tom,' said Sergeant Griffin, quite unexpectedly.

I must have dozed off. 'What do you think Bill's done?' I asked, as I rubbed the sleep from my eyes. We had arrived at the main entrance.

'Don't know, but I think it's damn lucky that you're not still living with him.'

'Do you think it's safe to go by the boatshed?'

'Why?'

'I think I might have left some stuff. One of my sweatshirts is missing and I can't find my gumboots.'

'I'll get back to you, Tom. It might not be safe with these characters about.'

Hazel stops me in the hall. 'They'll sleep like babies after all this excitement.'

'Hi, Haze.'

'You taking a break?'

'Yes,' I say, and the two of us laugh.

I follow Hazel out on to the veranda, past Papa, and around the corner towards the day bed. Hazel pauses to speak to an old woman. I don't recognise her. Maybe she is new. 'Someone has been looking for you,' Hazel says.

'Really?' The old woman looks blankly at me and then focuses back on Hazel. 'Who?'

'Young man, odd name,' says Hazel, and an image of Caleb Loeb pops into my head. 'Do you have a grandson?'

'A grandson…'

'I'll find out more and let you know,' says Hazel.

'Thanks, dear,' says the old woman, leaning back in her chair. She closes her eyes.

Hazel nods at me and we move off. 'Poor thing,' she says.

'Not a clue.'

'But she would know if she had a grandson, wouldn't she?'

'Hard to tell. She forgets where her room is.'

We walk past the day bed and down the ramp into the back garden. The swing seat is in the shade. We walk over and sit.

'But you have to be careful these days with identity fraud,' Hazel continues. 'Who knows why someone would pretend to have a granny, but the rules state that we have to do a thorough background check if the resident doesn't have the relative listed.'

'Pretend? You think the guy was making it up?'

My throat's really sore. I feel like I'm floating on Jonah's lilo. I try to open my eyes. I feel a long way from myself. Part of me doesn't even care.

'Should we bring in someone she knows?'

'I don't know. Worth a try, I guess.'

'Hazel,' I said, 'what about that woman's grandson. The one with the odd name. Did you meet him?'

'I can't tell you anything specific, Tom, because it's confidential. But generally speaking, a grandson is uncommon. It's usually an immediate family member: a child or sibling.

They've lost touch. Or they've had a falling-out and want to patch things up. The ones who come in person are almost always on the resident's list.'

'Has anyone like that ever visited Nana?'

'You mean, do you have an aunt or uncle you've never met?'

'Yeah, I guess.'

'Honestly, Tom, I can't remember off the top of my head. Your Nana's been here a long time. Let me think about it and see if anything drops in.'

Hazel's not usually vague. According to Papa, Hazel has an incredible memory. Papa reckons Hazel pretends to be silly so the rest of us don't flag her as smart.

Papa went to school with Hazel's father, Kevin. He says he remembers when Hazel was born. He and Kevin went to the pub and everyone kept buying them beers. They were so drunk by the time they got to the hospital to see the baby, they both passed out in the waiting room.

Kevin and his wife, Ellen, knew Hazel was special when she started reading at two. She started school at four. Papa says she's got an IQ higher than the Eiffel Tower and the teachers didn't know what to do with her. These days, Papa says, they would have stuck Hazel with the gifted kids, but back in the sixties it was more of a one-size-fits-all approach.

Inevitably, she got really bored, hung out with real losers, started stealing cars. By the time she was fourteen she had quit school and disappeared. Papa said he hadn't realised that the Hazel who worked at the Mavis Ornstein Home for the Elderly was Kevin and Ellen's Hazel.

But Nana knew. Nana reads the births, deaths and marriages section of the paper every day. One afternoon she spotted Ellen Croxly-Wrightson's death notice. 'Beloved wife of Kevin and mother of Hazel' it said.

Papa found Nana and Hazel in the reading room. Hazel was sitting at her desk, head in her hands, crying. Nana was standing next to her, gently patting her shoulder.

10

I just remembered why we named it the Rumbly. We had left early one morning, before sunrise. Bill had loaded the tinny onto the trailer the night before so we could leave straight away. But that meant I had no time for breakfast.

The drive to Fiske Point takes about twenty-five minutes and it takes at least that long again to drag the boat from the car park across the small sand dune to the creek. I was so hungry. My stomach started rumbling. It got louder once we started rowing upstream. I can't believe I had forgotten that.

I want to go to the boatshed. I'd like to find my sweatshirt and gumboots, but I really want to poke around Bill's stuff.

If it wasn't for the Minnow, I could sneak over on my own.

'Thanks a lot,' said the Minnow.

'Listen, I'm getting really sick of the lack of privacy,' I said to her.

'Well, I'm glad you can't go. Sergeant Griffin thinks it is unsafe.'

'I know. But I want to see if I can find out what Bill has been up to.' And if I could go alone I wouldn't have to explain what I was doing.

'We could go when Jonah's at the pie shop.'

'Alone also means without you,' I replied. Harsh but true.

'But Dr Patek would freak,' said the Minnow.

She was right, of course. I promised to be extra careful, and walking seven kilometres with the Minnow probably breaks that promise.

It was quiet for a moment. 'What if we borrowed the tinny?'

One thing was certain: the Minnow was smart.

I'd forgotten—but she had remembered—that the tinny was still tied up to the pier at the inlet. Bill had rowed to the inlet yesterday afternoon, and had escaped leaving the boat behind. What's more, I didn't think he would be in any hurry to collect it.

The tinny made getting to the boatshed a real possibility,

because rowing along the river to Jessops Creek is a shortcut. And Bill has his own pontoon, so there would be no risk of missing our stop.

Yep, the Minnow was brilliant.

'I heard that,' she said.

And annoying.

Later that night, the Minnow and I hatched a plan. It had to seem casual, nothing out of the ordinary. 'I'm just off to the inlet,' I practised.

The Minnow pretended to be Jonah. 'You should wait for me to take you.'

'It's okay,' I replied, 'Sergeant Griffin didn't say I couldn't go to the inlet.'

'Ahhh, but what about the FishMaster?' said the Minnow.

'Dammit,' I said, jumping out of the role-play. 'How will I get out of that one?' I drive Jonah nuts about the Fish-Master. He'd smell a rat if I didn't insist on taking it.

The Minnow and I lay there in the quiet, trying to think of a solution. But it was a waste of time.

I had no choice but to hassle Jonah about the skateboard. The Minnow and I agreed that I would suggest it first thing, over breakfast. If I used the Minnow's whiny voice, Jonah would probably offer to rig it up for me there and then.

'Night,' said the Minnow.

'Bed bugs bite,' I replied, patting my stomach.

But I was too churned up to sleep. I lay awake, listening to the noises outside, thinking how different my life would be if my family hadn't drowned.

At dawn, I thought of Sarah. She loved mornings and, ignoring my protests, would always climb into my bed as soon as she was awake. 'Tommy,' she'd whisper, resting her head on my chest, 'listen to the ferspers with me.'

Every morning began with snuggling and ferspers till Mum called us for breakfast. Sarah always sucked her thumb, and she refused to take her thumb out of her mouth to speak, so it took me years to realise that she was actually saying 'first birds'.

As it turns out, I didn't have to whine at all. Jonah said he had been thinking about the FishMaster and reckoned his old go-cart would be much sturdier than the skateboard. It only took Jonah a minute to find it stashed behind the garage door.

With the steering column unclipped and pulled forward, the go-cart was transformed into a tray with a long handle. Jonah checked the wheels while I got the tackle box from the house. Then we positioned the FishMaster at the front of the tray and secured it with an old belt in case I hit any bumps.

'Voila, madam!' Jonah said, when it was done.

'Mademoiselle. I'm not married.'

Jonah is not happy about me going to the inlet alone, but he isn't able to come up with an argument good enough to stop me. I wish I could tell him what I am planning to do, but he would tell his grandfather who would call Sergeant Griffin, so I say nothing, biding my time until he has left for school.

I watch him cycle down the drive, then wait an extra five minutes in case he comes back. Once it feels safe, I undo the strap and drag the FishMaster up the steps and back into the house. It's too big to fit under my bed, so I hide it behind the door.

I've decided to take the cart. It will come in handy if I find anything. It also means I can take a bottle of water and some food without having to carry them.

By nine o'clock, the Minnow and I are pushing off from the jetty. The cart was too awkward to lift into the boat so I left it behind. It means I'll have to carry stuff from the boatshed to the pontoon, but I'll deal with that when I get to it. The cart should be safe. I left it at the entrance to the jetty, tucked behind some bushes.

Rowing is not that easy with the Minnow, but I'm in no rush—the water's calm, the breeze is gentle. With each stroke, the tinny glides through the water.

It only takes about twenty minutes to reach the bend. Once I'm around it, the pontoon will be in sight. But that means I'll be visible. I realise I'll be less conspicuous if I row closer to the bank.

I turn the boat with one oar and row towards a group of trees about twenty metres this side of the bend. Now that I'm getting close, I start to feel nervous. What if Sergeant Griffin is right and it's not safe at the shed? What if the men at the jetty were hit men? What if Mr Handsome knows about the identikit? Will that mean they're looking for me? And what if Bill is there, hiding out? How will I explain myself if he catches me rummaging around?

I reach the trees. I lift the oars out of the water and into the boat. I need to think. I wish I'd brought the binoculars.

'Check under the seat,' says the Minnow.

Of course. Bill keeps a pair in the tinny. I stand carefully and lift the seat. There are two plastic containers. One is a holdall for spare fishing line, hooks and sinkers. It also contains a fishing knife and a rusty can opener. The other container holds the binoculars. I take them out, lower the seat and sit back down. In place of the strap, Bill has tied a piece of blue rope and I put it over my head. I check that the rope's knots are secure, then unbutton the case, remove the binoculars and take a look around.

First I look back towards the inlet. It seems remarkably

close. I scan the jetty. Then I sweep back and forth across the water. When I'm sure no one has followed me, I turn my attention towards the bend. Again, I check for any movement on the water. Just to be sure, I adjust the focus and search up and down the bank. Nothing.

I want to see exactly what I'm heading into, so rather than rowing in the normal way, I reverse my position on the seat so that I'm facing the boat's pointy end. Push rowing is odd, but not impossible. I lean forward and grasp the oars and swing them around in a wide arc so that they enter the water in front of me, rather than behind. I then reach forward, pushing the oars from front to back. It feels strange at first, but I soon find a rhythm.

Rounding the bend, I quickly lift the oars into the boat and use the binoculars to check my destination. There is no sign of anyone. I continue rowing, stopping once, only briefly, when something catches my eye.

I reach the pontoon without incident and tie the boat to one of the railings. I climb out of the tinny, walk up the floating ramp and across the pontoon to the steps. The steps are made of old tyres filled with gravel. The gravel makes a crunching sound which is quite loud, but not loud enough to be heard from the shed.

It is steeper than I remember, so I take my time.

'I should have left the binoculars in the tinny,' I say to

the Minnow when I realise they're still hanging around my neck. I look around for somewhere to stash them but it's no good; if I leave them here I'll never find them again. I'm annoyed with myself. The last thing I needed was to carry something unnecessarily. Thankfully, the rest of the walk to the shed is a flat dirt path.

'Shhh,' says the Minnow, stopping me in my tracks.

There are voices up ahead. Male voices. I crouch down and try to hear what they're saying, but they're too far away. I crawl a bit further up the path. The Minnow's extra weight means that crawling hurts my knees—but I'm too scared to stand up in case I give myself away.

I look around for somewhere to hide. To my left there is an entrance to a smaller track. It is quite overgrown and normally I would avoid it, but right now I need to get off the path in case they come this way.

The track turns away from the voices and seems to curve around in a semi-circle. I keep following it until it finishes behind the old chook pen. I'm not sure what to do next. My knees are aching and my legs are starting to cramp. I can't hear or see anyone, so I decide that it's safe to stand up. I stretch my legs and try to get my bearings. I think the chook pen was to the right of the boatshed but, if I remember correctly, it had an old rusty roof. This one looks new.

'Maybe there's a second chook pen,' suggests the Minnow.

'I don't think so,' I answer. 'Bill has replaced the old roof.'

I'm trying to decide whether to stay put or sneak back to the pontoon, when I'm interrupted.

'You're sure it's here?' says a man's voice.

'Positive,' replies a second voice, also male. Neither man sounds like Mr Handsome. There is a crunching sound and suddenly someone appears in the small clearing about ten metres in front of me.

Sarah and I hardly ever played hide-and-seek. Mum said it was an unfair game because Sarah always ended up in tears when she couldn't find me. I absolutely loved hiding and it never bothered me if Sarah wouldn't play, because I had just as much fun hiding on my own. Dad said I could hide in plain sight. I'm not sure how I did it, but I could stand flat against a wall and Mum would walk straight past and not notice I was there.

It took a few years of practice—and a lot of help from Papa—to hide from Dad. Papa said Dad's army training was our biggest hurdle. I tried asking Dad about it once, but he just walked away from me.

The trick, according to Papa, was to stay perfectly still

and *never* look at anyone directly. Eyes are so powerful, he told me, that other people can sense when they're being observed. 'But that's just the beginning,' said Papa. 'The only way you'll ever hide from your father is if you master the art of invisibility.'

I retraced my steps back along the track to the main path. Even though the men had left, I walked as quietly as possible. I kept expecting to hear Bill's voice.

The boatshed door was open. The place was in such a mess, a cat could lose its whiskers (Nana again). Upstairs, the loft was empty, except for the bed and an old rug that used to live on the veranda. It was a sad little room and it didn't look like it had been slept in since I left. It was hot and stuffy, so I unlatched one of the doors to let in some air.

'Jesus, you're a nosey little shit.'

It was Bill. Even though I was half expecting him, I got such a fright that I banged my head on the beam and a loud yell escaped from my mouth.

'That would've hurt,' he said.

I turned to face him. 'Papa says you're a sneaky bastard, and he's right,' I said, rubbing the sore spot. It felt like it was bleeding.

'Your Papa's dead,' Bill replied with a sneer.

'And you will be, too, if those men find you.'

'What do you know about them?'

'Nothing much,' I said, wishing I'd kept my mouth shut, 'except that they were here.'

'I'm more interested in what *you're* doing here,' he said.

That was the trouble with Bill. He wasn't easily distracted.

'I came to see you,' I lied.

'Liar,' he said, edging closer.

'Tell him you rowed over to see him, but those men were here, so you hid and waited for them to leave,' said Papa.

'You left the tinny at the inlet,' I said. 'I thought you might want it.'

'Even better,' said Papa.

'Thought you'd snoop around, you mean,' said Bill.

'Why would I snoop?' I said. 'I was just looking around because the men had left the place in such a mess. I was worried.'

Bill thought about this, weighed it up.

'What's with the go-cart?' he asked.

The question caught both Papa and me off guard. Bill must have hiked to the jetty with the intention of collecting the tinny. Shit.

'It's all right,' said Papa, reading my thoughts. 'Bet he doesn't know you tried to bring it with you.'

'The go-cart is Jonah's idea,' I said, keeping my voice steady. 'It's my new wheels for the FishMaster.'

Bill gave me a look that meant he needed more information.

'So I can walk to the inlet without Jonah,' I explained.

I watched him digest this.

'Well, your fancy-pants tackle box has been stolen,' said
Bill.

My heart was beating so hard, it felt as though the
Minnow was kicking me in the chest. 'I left the FishMaster
at home,' I said, explaining away the empty go-cart. 'I hadn't
planned on fishing today, just taking the tinny out. Thought
I'd give the go-cart a road test.' I gave him my best smile.
Everything's fine, my smile said. 'Anyway, I'm glad you're
here,' I added, still smiling. 'Those men were pretty hectic.'

Bill just stared at me. I could tell he wasn't buying it.

'What's with the binoculars?'

Shit, shit, shit.

'Sightseeing,' suggested Papa. It was pretty lame, but I
had nothing else.

'I took my time rowing here,' I said. 'Dr Patek says I have
to take it easy. So I did a bit of sightseeing.'

Nana says lying's not so hard if you wrap it around the
truth.

We were interrupted by the sound of car tyres skidding
to a halt on the other side of the boatshed. The engine cut.
A door slammed.

'Tom!' It was Sergeant Griffin.

Bill turned on me with his angry face. 'You tell that idiot you haven't seen me.'

'What about those men?' I asked.

'You haven't seen anyone. Okay?'

'Okay,' I answered.

'Don't fuck-up, Tom. Now get downstairs and don't let him come up.'

I could hug Sergeant Griffin.

11

'It's called the tipping point,' says Jonathan Whiting, slowing to thirty as we enter the roundabout. 'It is a particular number, a critical mass. It is the moment when enough people buy something or like something or use something that propels that something into play.'

'Uh huh,' I say. 'You mean like Coke?'

'Coke is a difficult example because it is so heavily advertised. Think of something else, something unusual, not necessarily mainstream.'

Jonathan Whiting and I have started having conversations on the way to the Mavis Ornstein Home for the Elderly. He knows heaps of really weird and interesting stuff. Papa would get upset if he knew about it, so I haven't told him.

'There was this kid at school, before the flood. Brandon Holloway. Brandon had this weird way of drawing people. He would always start at the feet and work up to the head. All the boys in his group started copying him. I think at first they did it for fun, but by the end of term the whole art class was doing it.'

'What about the rest of the school?'

'Ummm,' I said, pressing my forefinger to my mouth. 'Don't remember. We all knew about it, but I don't remember any of the other classes following suit.' I learned 'following suit' from Jonathan. He says it all the time. 'Would the whole school have to join in to reach the tipping point?' I ask, replaying the question in my mind just to hear it again.

'Not necessarily,' Jonathan replies. 'Think of a wheelbarrow full of concrete. You put in the sand, gravel and cement, and then you add water until everything's wet and well mixed. It takes a certain amount of water, doesn't it, before the mix is right?'

'I've never made concrete.'

'Okay. But are you with me?'

This is what Jonathan does. He gets me thinking about a subject. He calls it the 'primary engagement'. He then throws in something that seems totally irrelevant. He calls this the 'expansion point'. Concrete is his cue for me to expand my thinking. Jonathan says our minds are magnificent, and not only do they cope with the unexpected they thrive on it.

'Concrete is like a cake. The ingredients need to be exact for it to work,' I say, thinking out loud.

'Exact?'

'Yes. Sponge cakes require the exact ingredients.' Mum told me the secret to the perfect sponge was precision.

'Go on. Remember not to limit your thinking.'

I stop for a moment. Dad used to say his best ideas were never planned.

'I have the exact amount of water in a bucket. The bucket leans over the cement mixer and the Brandon amount spills in. When one of Brandon's friends starts drawing the feet first, the bucket tips in a bit more water. Another friend joins in, another and another, until, whoosh, the bucket has tipped past the point of no return and all the water falls into the mixer.'

'Excellent. What's your reasoning?'

'I'm thinking that the tipping point was the size of Brandon's group of friends. It was large enough to produce the trend that caused the class to embrace Brandon's style.'

'Tom, I think you've made your case.'

'So, Tom,' says Sergeant Griffin, unclipping his seatbelt and turning to face me. He has driven me to Jonah's house, even though I said I would rather row home.

'So…?' I answer.

'Tom, don't play games. What were you doing at the boatshed?'

'Sorry, Sergeant Griffin.' I'm still trying to figure out how he knew I was there. 'Please don't tell Dr Patek.'

'Listen to me, young lady,' he says, jabbing his finger in the air. 'This has nothing to do with Dr Patek and everything to do with you not cooperating with the police.' Sweat beads on his chin. He loosens his tie and pulls at the collar of his shirt.

'I have cooperated, Sergeant Griffin. Why can't I go to the boatshed?'

'Because you're a *fifteen-year-old pregnant girl*,' he says, almost shouting, 'and you could be in danger. We still have no idea who those men are—and Bill has been missing since they turned up.' He sucks in a deep breath, then exhales loudly.

'Sorry, Sergeant Griffin.' I unclip my seatbelt.

'Listen, Tom,' Sergeant Griffin says, in a voice that is more familiar. 'I hate to get angry with you, especially after everything you've gone through. But this is my town and you're my responsibility. You understand?'

I nod, yes. I have to get out of the car before I suffocate, and I push open the door and haul myself out. Sergeant Griffin leans across and catches my eye. 'Don't make things any harder than they need to be, Tom.'

As I walk down the drive to Jonah's house, I realise the binoculars are still around my neck.

Jonathan Whiting used to be a lawyer. He retired when he turned seventy, but he still works as a consultant to keep his brain active.

'I have a task for you,' he says as we pull into the car park. Tasks can be anything. One time he handed me a Rubik's Cube and asked if I could fix it. I thought I was doing him a favour.

'N.i.b.l.i.c.k,' he says, spelling a word. 'I want you to look it up and give it an origin.'

I grab my notebook and write down 'niblick' and 'origin' and wait for more instructions.

'One week from today,' he says, 'I'm playing in the Old Silks golf tournament. I'll be away eight days. Think you can find another chauffeur for a week?'

'I'll ask around,' I say, closing the notebook. 'I didn't know you played golf.'

'There are probably lots of things you don't know about me. Just like there are lots of things I don't know about you.'

Old and weird moment. My cue to get out of the car.

'Thanks, Jonathan,' I say. 'I'll be with Nana in about halfa.'

'You're not going there now?'

'I want to talk to Hazel first.'

I can hear voices, far away.

I let my mind drift.

I feel weightless, calm.

Someone is humming.

'Tommy? Is that you?'

'I've been sleeping like a baby.'

'That's the ticket,' says Clare.

'I've been thinking about a turtle.'

'Don't know. We used to get the occasional. Hang on.'
Clare walks out the back. 'Marge,' she says—and I realise
she's talking to Mrs Blanket—'Tom's here asking about
turtles.'

My eyes drift up to the carp tank. Mrs Blanket hasn't
replaced Oscar. I don't think her heart is in it.

I feel a bit dizzy. Mrs Blanket has a customer chair in the
aisle next to the guinea pig hutch. I walk over and sit down.
There's a small brown guinea pig asleep on a heart-shaped
pillow. It's one of those little pillows that florists attach
to bouquets of flowers. Mrs Blanket's Oscar flowers. As I
stare at the little guinea pig, he stretches and yawns and
rolls off the pillow onto his back. He has a small wisp of

white under his chin. 'Hi, Rumbly,' I say.

Fielder's Pets and Supplies hasn't been part of my Saturday ritual since Dr Patek introduced the moderate exercise rule. But, as of today, James Wo now comes by the house on Saturday mornings rather than after school on Fridays. Friday afternoons had begun to clash with school meetings. Jonah arrived home yesterday afternoon with a message from James Wo regarding the change.

'What if it doesn't suit me?' I said to Jonah when he relayed the message.

'Don't be annoying, Tom.'

'I'm serious,' I said. 'What if I'd made plans?

'Have you?'

'What?'

'Made plans.'

'That's not the point. Does he expect you to cycle all the way back to school and give him an answer?'

'Don't shoot the messenger,' said Jonah.

'What's that supposed to mean?'

James Wo arrived this morning at nine. I had just had my shower, so he waited outside for a bit. I might have made plans. I might have been planning to go back to the boatshed.

'You can come in now,' I called, once I was dressed.

We sat at the kitchen table. He reviewed my work and

outlined the lesson plan for the following week. Then he offered to drive me into town.

'Do you drive into town every Saturday?' I asked.

'You're like an open book, Tom.'

It has been over a month since I left the Mater Women's Hospital in West Wrestler. Dr Frank has checked me over and is on the phone to Dr Patek. They're both happy with my progress. The Minnow is coming along nicely, positioned head down, ready for her exit. Dr Patek and Dr Frank assume this is stressful for me, but it isn't. The Minnow is quite happy. She and I have reached an understanding. She has even told me the date: December twenty-six. Dr Patek says I'm due on the seventh of January. She has also warned me that first babies can be up to two weeks late.

Not the Minnow. She is thirty-one weeks and counting.

> **niblick** *nib'lick, n.* a golf club with a heavy head
> with wide face, used for lofting—a number eight
> or nine iron. [Origin uncertain].

'Haze, you busy?'

'Always, darl. What's up?'

I know nothing about golf, but Hazel is a fanatic.

'I need to know some stuff about a golf club,' I say, and

I show her the dictionary entry.

'This an assignment for school?' she asks.

'No. Jonathan Whiting gives me tasks.'

Hazel looks at me strangely. 'It's Kosher, right?'

'Sure. He's sweet. I live with his grandson. He's in love with my Nana. I think he's taken me under his wing.'

Niblick, I wrote, is a word-cousin of nitwit. Nitwit is slang for idiot or blockhead. It means literally to not (nit) have wit. Niblick is army slang for nobility. It is used to describe English officers whose position is granted through noblesse, rather than officers who earn their rank through hard work. Niblick refers to an officer who is found wanting, unprepared for the demands of army life, ill-equipped to the point of stupidity in the face of pressure.

Niblick is believed to have been transferred across to golf, in particular, to the niblick nine iron, in honour of a group of nine officers who played a five-day golf tournament while posted in the Falkland Islands. This, I said melodramatically, is unconfirmed.

'You made this up?' asked Jonathan Whiting.

'Uh huh,' I answered, smiling.

'All of it?'

'All except nitwit. That's a real word.'

'Brilliant, Tom. How did you know the task was an

exercise in imagination?'

'Because you said to *give* niblick an origin.'

'Well done twice,' he said. 'For listening and originality.'

'Thanks, Jonathan.'

I found a stand-in chauffeur through Hazel: a guy everyone calls Peter Perfect, although the 'perfect' bit is just a nickname. Peter Perfect's brother, Marcus, also lives at the Mavis Ornstein Home for the Elderly, in the nursing-home wing. Peter visits him every second day.

'Come and meet him,' says Hazel, holding my elbow and steering me down the hall. 'He lives near Jonah's house, and he says it's no problem.'

We walk past the kitchen, the staffroom and the dispensary, across a courtyard and through a security-coded door into the hospital building. We take the lift upstairs, and walk past the empty nurses' station to room seventeen. The door is ajar.

'His brother's in a coma,' whispers Hazel. 'You ready for this?' she asks.

I'm about to respond when Hazel knocks and enters, pulling me in with her.

'Peter, this is Tom,' says Hazel. 'Tom is Valerie Wolkoff's granddaughter.'

'Oh, yes,' says Peter Perfect, crossing one leg over the

other and looking altogether too neat. 'Tom,' he says and pulls the chair next to him a bit closer, 'come and sit down and let's get acquainted.'

I look across at Hazel. She smiles and mouths the words 'it's only for a week'.

'When are you going to tell Jonah about Rumbly?' Jonathan Whiting asks me as he pulls the cream Bentley into a parking spot outside Fielder's Pets and Supplies.

'I'm waiting for the right moment,' I answer.

It's been over a week since I met Rumbly. Jonathan says he doesn't mind the detour, although his question tells me it can't go on forever. 'We don't have to drop by every day,' I say.

'Tom, it's fine,' he says. 'It's almost on the way. I just think you need to tell Jonah. Then you can take Rumbly home.'

Jonathan likes Rumbly. Yesterday he bought him a hutch. And he's right: I really ought to tell Jonah. I haven't said anything because I feel guilty. I should've said something earlier…and by earlier, I mean before I bought Rumbly.

'Do you want me to tell him?' asks Jonathan.

'Okay,' I say. 'That'd be great.'

12

I am dead to the world, dreaming of Sarah and Mum and me. We are walking along the sand spit at Fiske Point and for the first time ever there's not the slightest breeze. I feel so happy. I'm smiling.

'Look at that,' says Sarah. She is walking on our left, the bay side, but she is pointing across to the ocean. Mum and I stop walking and turn to our right. The ocean is dark but clear, and swimming alongside us, almost close enough to touch, are three dolphins. They swim past and disappear.

'Quick,' says Sarah. 'Catch up or we'll lose them.' Sarah lets go of Mum's hand and runs ahead.

Mum and I continue walking. Sarah turns to look at us.

'C'mon, you two,' she shouts across the sand. Her words

float towards us. Mum squeezes my hand reassuringly and I look up at her, but the sun is in my eyes, obliterating her face.

Obliterate was yesterday's word. The thesaurus gives alternatives like annihilate, delete, destroy and eradicate, but the dictionary's entry is much calmer: it says simply 'to blot out'. I find it interesting that the thesaurus and dictionary can have such disparate perspectives. My thesaurus doesn't have a listing for disparate. I'm a bit disappointed about that.

'Slow down,' Mum calls to Sarah. Mum and I have no chance of catching up. I'm not worried. I'm just a kid.

'Sarah will have to stop when she reaches the point,' I say, sensing Mum's concern.

The sun is shimmering across the sand. It is becoming hard to focus, the glare is making my eyes water. If Sarah runs into the shimmer we'll lose sight of her.

'Mum,' I say.

'I know,' she answers. 'I can't see her either.'

Betsy Groot has died. Hazel catches Jonathan and me as soon as we arrive. Nana, she tells us, is inconsolable.

There is a long and quite beautiful gardenia hedge that runs along the road frontage of the grand acreage that is the Mavis Ornstein Home for the Elderly. Gardenia *granda flora*, in the form of hundreds of plants packed side by side and two metres tall. Once inside the property, a fledgling version of the hedge continues. Knee high shrubs have been planted on either side of the drive, all the way to the main administration building. The entrance to the visitors' car park is the only break, but the gap is hardly discernable given the double row of plants at the inward curve which, when fully grown, will conceal the car park altogether.

Papa uses the hedge as a living message board, nipping buds and deadheading at precise intervals so that today, for example, BETSY GROOT is spelled out in perfectly formed creamy-white blooms. Jonathan didn't notice, but for the Minnow and me, it was impossible to miss.

Funerals are a constant at the Mavis Ornstein Home for the Elderly. A fact of life, Nana says, without a trace of irony. But this one will be particularly sad. Nana and Betsy have been close friends for over forty years.

We find Nana in her room. She has a box of tissues on her lap and she is holding a framed photo of eight women dressed in regulation white. Four of the women are seated, the other four are standing behind them, and all eight are beaming at the camera. The photo has been taken on a bowling green, and on the ground in front of them is a rather large collection of trophies.

I know why Nana is crying. In the past two years, Amy Carpenter, Flo Allan, Enid Habib and now Betsy Groot have all died. Half the winning team.

'I need a new photo,' says Nana, as we enter. 'This one is just too sad.' She places the frame face down on the card table and blows her nose. 'Pour me a gin will you, Jonathan?' she asks, holding her empty tumbler towards him at full reach. 'And for god's sake, Jono, make it worthy of being called a bloody drink.'

Nana and I watch as Jonathan Whiting pours a hefty gin. Nana winks at me as though she and I are in cahoots. She would be disappointed to know that Jonathan is not alone in thinking she drinks too much. But I say nothing.

Jonathan screws the lid back on the bottle, tucks the bottle behind the sofa, and hands Nana her favourite tipple. 'Cheers big ears,' she says, lifting the glass in a salute before taking a large swig. 'Tom, darling, pass me a coaster.'

Generally speaking, when Nana loses a friend, it is through old age. I envy her that.

Whenever I can't sleep, I count sheep. My friend Tracey-Ann (from before the flood) taught me a special method. 'You can't just count sheep, one, two, three,' she said. 'You have to create your own flock.'

Tracey-Ann was adamant that counting sheep was the best cure for sleeplessness. The special method, she said, had been handed down for generations and her whole family swore by it.

'First,' she said, 'you have to imagine a flock. It doesn't matter how big, in fact, the bigger the better.'

'Hundreds?' I asked her.

'Sure, if you want,' she said. 'There's no limit.'

We're lying on the floor of the tree house. We've been here since lunchtime.

'Imagine the sheep, grazing in a paddock,' she said. She paused and looked at me. 'Close your eyes, Tom,' she said in her terse voice, 'and pretend it's night-time and you're in bed.' She waited a beat.

'Now, this is important,' she continued. 'They're not taking any notice of you. They're grazing. You're observing.'

I lay perfectly still, imagining my sheep and waiting for her next instruction.

'Imagine every detail,' she said after a lengthy pause. 'What do the sheep look like? Are they all white, or do they have black faces? Are they woolly or recently shorn? Are they noisy or quiet? Are there any lambs? Is the paddock lush and green or brown with winter grass?'

'You're serious?'

'Trust me, the more clearly you imagine it, the more potent the sheeping-pill,' she said, and she turned to face me. 'Get it?'

'Oh, yes, *sheeping*-pill,' I said, with emphasis. Tracey-Ann looked pleased.

Actually, it was easier than it sounded. When I bothered to focus, I realised the paddock had been there all the time. And I had a few hundred sheep, heads down, grazing, content. Okay, I thought, what's next?

'That's all you do on the first night,' answered Tracey-Ann. 'I'll come over tomorrow afternoon.'

I was sure she was dragging it out just to get another one of Mum's lunches. But I didn't care.

Everyone at the Mavis Ornstein Home for the Elderly designs their own farewell. The first Tuesday of every second month is set aside specifically for 'the last hurrah'. Residents have to book ahead to make one-on-one appointments with Hazel. Some of them take it quite seriously, logging every detail and making new appointments for the most minor alterations. Every aspect of their funeral is thought out, discussed, written down. Sometimes residents even plan their own wake.

Betsy Groot was a lapsed Catholic. Nana said she adored this title and took every opportunity to use it to describe herself. That being said, she had planned a traditional service, even requesting the Catholic priest from Hillier Saint Martin in West Wrestler to deliver the eulogy.

The Mavis Ornstein Home for the Elderly has its own chapel. The Jeffrey Gallico Chapel is named after Mavis Ornstein's closest friend. It is hidden behind a hedge, a short walk from the common room.

Nana and the remaining bowling girls are seated at the front, dressed in their whites. I am directly behind them, sandwiched between Papa and Betsy.

The air smells of incense, gardenias and gin.

'Now imagine you're standing in the holding yard,' said Tracey-Ann.

It was the following day, and Tracey-Ann was talking me through the next step. She'd arrived after lunch. Mum said I shouldn't be so quick to judge people.

'The sheep,' she said, 'which last night were grazing, are now looking at you...' I pictured them raising their heads 'because, in a moment, you're going to open the gate.' Tracey-Ann made this sound quite dramatic.

I realised my paddock was missing a gate. I plonked one in.

'But before you do,' Tracey-Ann interrupted my train of thought, 'you need to decide whether you'll choose the sheep yourself or invite them in and take pot luck.'

'What's the difference?' I asked. I didn't want to go into this unprepared.

She sat up and looked at me long and hard. 'Choosing is harder because you have to manoeuvre the sheep through the gate yourself. This can take ages.'

She delivered this in the manner of a late-night news-reader.

'Inviting them is easier,' she continued. 'You just wait for the curious ones to move into the holding yard by themselves.'

I thought about this for a few seconds.

'I think I'll choose,' I said, rather happy with my decision to go against the tide.

'Cool,' said Tracey-Ann. 'Although you might live to regret it.'

Nana moves to the front. It is her turn to speak. She clears her throat and looks directly at the space on my right. 'Betsy Groot,' she begins, 'will be missed.'

'She can see us, you know,' says Papa, leaning forward and speaking directly to Betsy.

'I thought so,' Betsy replies.

'Maybe you'll have better luck,' he says. It is fleeting, but all the sadness of Papa's loneliness is captured in that moment.

They stare at each other as though I'm not there.

One of the really big differences between living with Jonah and living with Bill is that Jonah is hardly ever moody. Even when he is tired or a bit crabby, he doesn't take it out on me. For example, this morning he woke with a cold, but he didn't complain. When we realised we had run out of milk, he didn't get upset: he jumped on his bike and cycled four kilometres to the dairy and came home with two litres, still warm from milking. When I told him he was amazing, he just shrugged his shoulders and said I would do the same. But I'm not sure. I think I would get the shits.

The other night I had a chocolate craving, and Jonah brought me the jar of Nutella and a spoon and said that he didn't mind if I ate the lot (even though Nutella on toast is his favourite thing for breakfast). I made sure I left him some. When he noticed, he said, 'Tom, you're so thoughtful,' and he meant every word.

If Bill had said something like that, it would be full of sarcasm.

I find myself making comparisons.

Jonah is an amazing friend. He would be the one thing I'd take if I were stuck on a desert island.

'Aren't you forgetting someone?' said the Minnow.

Jonathan told Jonah about Rumbly, and he doesn't seem to mind. Jonathan delivered the hutch this morning, and Jonah and I have set it up on the veranda. We put in hay and guinea pig food and a water dispenser, and an old beanie of mine in case he gets cold. Rumbly seems happy with the arrangement.

Mrs Blanket let him keep the little heart pillow and right now he is lying across it, fast asleep.

'Rumbly's a really cool name,' says Jonah. The two of us are sitting on the veranda watching Rumbly sleep.

'Thanks,' I say.

'Where did you get it?'

'Oh, I don't remember,' I answer.

I'm not going to tell Jonah another Bill-and-me story. I'm done talking about Bill.

13

Mum lets go of my hand and starts to run.

'Sarah!' she calls. There is a panicky sound in her voice.

I want to run but my legs are as heavy as stone. I fall forwards onto my hands and knees and try to crawl. The breeze has picked up and it is blowing sand into my eyes. I can hardly move, barely see. 'Mum,' I yell, squinting into the abyss, 'don't leave me.'

I feel a hand on my shoulder.

'Tom.'

It's Jonah. He is gently shaking me awake.

'Tom,' he says again. 'You were having a nightmare.'

I start to cry. Before the flood, I always felt relieved when I woke from a bad dream.

'It's okay, Tom,' says Jonah. 'I have them too.'

'Jonathan, do you think it's possible to compress time?'

We are having our usual chat while driving to the Mavis Ornstein Home for the Elderly. 'Time certainly feels compressed when you get to my age,' answers Jonathan, smiling to himself. 'Years disappear in the blink of an eye.'

'I was sort of wondering about dreams.'

'Dreams are an altogether different proposition,' he says. 'I'm not sure whether they compress time or simply alter our perception of it.'

I always use my thesaurus and dictionary together, not in any particular order, although on this occasion I turn to the dictionary first. Perception is one of those words with a dictionary definition that is meticulous, and a bit overwhelming, so I decide to check if there is an entry in the thesaurus. It is a rewarding sight; the thesaurus has a listing for perception, perceive, perceptible and perceptive. I read them all; then I reread the dictionary entry.

'Here we are,' says Jonathan, as we're pulling into the car park.

'Jonathan,' I say, as I pack my books into my old schoolbag. 'I won't be needing these today. Can I leave them in the car?'

'I don't know how you do it,' he says, turning to look at

me and using his eyebrows to indicate the books on my lap. 'I'd be as sick as a dog.'

Sarah used to get carsick. She would hang her head out the car window. She said that the wind made her feel better. Mum always let her sit in the front. I couldn't see how sitting in the front seat could make a difference to her stomach.

Nana pauses. She doesn't like interruptions, and this one seems to be my fault. Jonathan and Mavis are standing in the aisle, looking at me.

'It's all right dear,' says Mavis. 'Just shuffle along.'

Easier said than done, however, as Betsy appears reluctant to budge. Understandable, given that it is her funeral, but if she doesn't vacate her seat in about three seconds she'll suffer the indignity of either Jonathan or Mavis sitting in her lap.

I jab Papa in the ribs.

'C'mon Betsy, I'll show you the hedge,' says Papa, jumping to his feet. 'Sorry sport,' he says to me, 'I was miles away.'

Betsy smiles and pats my arm. 'Thanks for coming, dear. It's been a lovely service. That priest was wonderful, the things he said.' She kisses me on the cheek, then squeezes past the Minnow and follows Papa out of the chapel. They duck between the columns and disappear into the garden.

Relieved, I shuffle across into Papa's spot at the end of the bench and Mavis and Jonathan take their seats.

'This is Valerie Wolkolf's granddaughter, Tom,' says Hazel, holding my elbow. Hazel is always around old people, so holding elbows is second nature to her.

Hazel is introducing me to one of Betsy's relatives. Everyone is in the common room and, in line with Betsy's request, we're drinking tequila margaritas. I'm in my eighth month. I've checked with the Minnow and we can't see how one margarita could hurt, so I've got a large salt-encrusted drink in my hand, and I think it's upsetting some of the funeral guests.

'Tom,' continues Hazel, 'this is Annabel, Betsy's grand-daughter.' Hazel turns and leaves. Our cue to open the conversation.

'We heard about the flood,' says Annabel. 'We're so sorry. Our grandmother told us you lost your whole family.' She keeps saying 'we' and 'us' and it is a bit weird.

'I still have Nana,' I say.

Annabel is beautiful. She has long black hair and dark skin. Her eyes are such a dark brown that it is hard to distinguish the pupil. There are small bubbles escaping from her shoulders. Tiny little bubbles, almost blue in colour, although I realise that's probably an illusion. They are most likely clear.

'Of course. Your Nana. Betsy talks about her all the time,' says Annabel.

'Talked,' interrupts a male voice.

Annabel's eyes widen for the briefest moment. She is looking at me, almost staring. 'That's my cousin,' she says.

I wonder if he is part of 'we'.

Annabel turns around and mutters something under her breath to a male version of herself. They are so alike they could be twins.

She turns back to me. Smiles. Then she tilts her head a fraction, moves her eyes to the side and speaks over her shoulder. 'Get me a drink, would you?'

The cousin looks from Annabel to me. His eyes are cold.

'Sure,' he says. 'But you won't like the salt.'

Annabel turns back to me and rolls her eyes.

'Then see if you can get me a sugar-rim. Otherwise, just a clean glass,' she says. Her eyes remain fixed on me. Strangely, it doesn't feel uncomfortable.

I'm guessing Annabel is twenty-something. She has the most perfect skin. And tiny fish scales on the sides of her neck. I imagine her hair hides them most of the time.

She is wearing a long dress the colour of paua shell, with the thinnest iridescent shoulder straps. She isn't wearing any jewellery except for a pearl ring on her right index finger, which she plays with while she talks.

'I think Annabel is a mermaid,' whispers the Minnow.

I know what she means. I've never met anyone who belonged in the ocean more than Annabel. But that myth about mermaids being able to walk on land is just fantasy. They can never leave the sea.

On the way back to Jonah's house, Jonathan brings up our earlier conversation.

'Once, and I have no idea when,' he begins, 'I listened to a radio program about sleep. I had forgotten all about it, but something that minister said jogged my memory.'

Jonathan can be extremely formal. He has rules about what constitutes a conversation. I have to say something now.

'What did the program say?' I ask.

'It was a documentary on sleep disorders. It cited the case of a man who had gone to sleep as usual, but who dreamed an entire lifetime in the one night. Apparently the dream began with his birth and ended eighty or so years later with his death. When interviewed, he said it was the most terrifying experience of his life. Apparently, day after day, year after year, he was at all times conscious that he was trapped in a dream. The whole ordeal rendered him rather fearful of sleep.' Jonathan taps the steering wheel with his thumbs. It is one of the things he does.

'Understandable, I suppose,' he continues, more to

himself, than to me. 'The poor man must have dreaded the prospect of having it happen a second time.' His thumbs have settled into a steady drum rhythm.

'Jonathan, if he'd killed himself—jumped off a building or something—wouldn't the fright have woken him up?'

'Good question, Tom,' Jonathan replies. 'I don't remember that being discussed.'

It's a cold Saturday afternoon. I'm mooching around at Fielder's Pets and Supplies. Mrs Blanket is away for the week (visiting her daughter), and Clare is looking after the shop. I am having a conversation with a seahorse called the Professor, who, it turns out, is a Buddhist. I've just finished telling him about the man who had the dream that lasted eighty years.

'Fish don't distinguish reality as separate,' says the Professor, after thinking it over for about ten minutes. 'In fact, it would be safe to say that we dream our reality, quite literally.'

'Does that mean you never actually sleep?' I ask.

'This is hard to answer.'

He appears to have drifted off in thought. So I wait.

'In simple terms,' he says suddenly, 'fish are always dreaming, but we don't experience sleep as such.'

He swims closer to the glass. I think he is staring at me.

'For example,' he continues, fluttering in a slow turn, 'you dream in your sleep. If you dream while awake, it's called hallucinating. If you're awake within in a dream, it's called lucid dreaming. These are quite different from the aquatic experience.'

I try to take it all in. A customer walks into the shop. The screen door smacks against the bell. I turn to look, but it is no one I know. The stranger walks over to the bird section and picks up a bag of birdseed, has a brief conversation with Clare and pays for the seed. The screen door smacks against the bell as he exits.

'Humans can't conceive of life as a continuous state.' The Professor stops fluttering. I watch as he drifts slowly to the bottom of the tank. 'I imagine the need for sleep interrupts the human's ability to understand the continuity of life.'

He is motionless.

The pet shop is silent except for the low hum of the fish tanks.

I'm not sure I understand.

'Most of you don't,' he answers, reading my mind.

With that, he swims an awkward circuit of his tank, stopping just above the shipwreck. Mrs Blanket has a thing for shipwrecks. Every tank has one. Some are big, some little. The Professor's shipwreck is quite grand; it has a filter that emits a small stream of bubbles. I wait for him to say something else. Finally, he speaks.

'That man who dreamed a lifetime,' he says, 'is the

closest you'll get to my reality.' And with that he turns and flutters to the back of the tank.

The Professor makes me realise how much I miss Oscar.

I have organised to meet Jonah at three o'clock outside Saint Joseph's Anglican Church. It is a tiny red-brick building with an orange tiled roof and a front garden full of roses. Mum loved it. She said it was The Crossing's prettiest building. She and Dave McKewen used to be on the garden committee. They tended the roses.

Mum used to strike rose cuttings in a little raised garden she called the nursery. Dad built the garden with bricks he scrounged from Bunter and Davis. He built it up to knee level, which Mum said was the perfect height—and Dad said was damn lucky because he kept going until he had run out of bricks. Mum's favourite rose was the harlequin and her second favourite was anything with a scent.

Jonah is late, or I'm early. So I spend the time walking from rose to rose, trying to figure out which of the scented roses are Mum's and which are Dave McKewen's. One of the harlequins almost has a perfume, but I think it's just borrowing some smell from its neighbour.

The church garden is full of colour. A few men from the Survivors tend it now. They made a little plaque to acknowledge the garden's former caretakers. I used to think it was a good idea, but—looking at it now—it makes Mum and Dave look like lovers.

Finally, Jonah arrives and we sit on the steps and share a sausage roll and a spinach pie and wait for Jonathan to collect us. It's quiet. The Minnow is moving. I take Jonah's hand and place it on my belly.

'I wish you were the Minnow's father,' I say to Jonah.

'Me too,' says Jonah.

'Me three,' says the Minnow.

'What did you say?' asks Jonah.

'He heard me!' says the Minnow.

Jonah's expression can only be described as startled.

'Are you serious, Jonah? Can you hear the Minnow?'

'Say yes, Jonah, say yes!' the Minnow shouts.

'I think so, yes,' he says. 'It's is a bit weird, though, isn't it?'

'Totally,' I answer.

'Absolutely,' says the Minnow.

Jonah starts to laugh. 'I thought you were crazy,' he says.

'I know.'

'Bet you're *astonished*,' says the Minnow, showing off.

'Get her to say something else,' says Jonah. His normally passive face is almost contorted with a mix of excitement and disbelief.

'Oh,' I say, as I realise what's just happened. 'It's totally random, Jonah. I can't *get* her to speak.'

'Oh, right, of course,' he says. '…it's just that you talk to her all the time.'

'Jonah, all pregnant mothers do that. It's called bonding. It doesn't mean we're having a conversation. But every now and then I actually hear her say something. And, just now, you heard her too.'

'So, he can't hear me now?' asks the Minnow, the frustration in her voice rising to a squeak. But she doesn't require an answer; Jonah's lack of reaction says it all.

We sit, side by side, thinking. Minutes tick by.

'I wonder what's taking Jonathan so long,' I say. Jonah and I gaze down the street, his hand on my belly. No sign of the car.

'Can we keep it our secret?' asks Jonah.

'Absolutely,' I answer, borrowing the Minnow's new favourite word.

It's quiet. We've finished the food, so there's nothing to do now but wait for our lift. I decide I may as well pick some flowers. Jonah pulls me to my feet.

'Coming?' I ask him.

'No, I'll wait here,' he answers, sitting back down on the step.

I collect the secateurs from the post box and start with one of the Harlequins.

'Jonah,' I say, 'can I ask you something?'

'Sure,' he says. He changes his mind about the step and moves over to the low brick wall so that he can sit facing me.

'It's about Bill,' I say. 'Should I tell Sergeant Griffin that I've been seeing him?'

'Tom! What do you mean?'

'Don't get your knickers in a knot,' I reply, wishing I'd kept my thoughts to myself, 'I just see him sometimes. At the inlet, usually, but the other day he was at the boatshed.'

'What, you mean you're *seeing* him?' Jonah's face is actually going red.

'No, no, no,' I blurt when I realise what he's asking. I make a two-fingered pointing gesture from my eyes to his. 'I *see* him,' I clarify. Jonah nods. But I feel hot, flustered, almost sick.

'We don't arrange to meet,' I continue. 'It's not like before when he'd collect me from your house. But he knows my habits. He knows how easy it is to find me. So, yes, when I'm at the inlet, he turns up. It's not like I have a choice.'

'So when he was there the other day—and those two men with the rifles—you and he were...fishing?'

'Yes.' It sounded weird. 'You don't understand, Jonah.' I couldn't expect Jonah to understand—I didn't even understand it. 'Sometimes I miss him and it's good to catch up. Other times he just appears.' Like a bad egg.

'Then, yes, you should tell Sergeant Griffin.'

'But I'm scared, Jonah.'

'Sergeant Griffin's a pussycat, Tom.'

'No, Jonah, I'm scared of saying anything against Bill.'

Jonah looks at me. He can see the fear on my face. Just showing him how I feel, not hiding it for once, is terrifying.

'Then we'll speak to Grandpa. He's a lawyer and he has to keep what you tell him confidential. He'll know the best way to handle Bill.'

'Okay. But let me think about it first.'

14

'Sergeant Griffin is looking for you,' says Papa.

Papa has a habit of speaking to me whenever he pleases. At this very moment I'm fast asleep, but that doesn't seem to matter to him.

'Tom,' he says, raising his voice. His tone tells me he's getting agitated. If I ignore him for much longer he'll lean down next to my ear and whistle.

'Papa,' I say, keeping my eyes closed and trying my hardest not to wake up, 'I'm in the middle of a dream about Mum.'

'Sorry sport,' he says, 'but I just passed Griffin on his way here and he was speeding.'

'Speeding?' I sit bolt upright. Sergeant Griffin only ever

speeds if he's in a hurry. I know that sounds like I'm stating the obvious, but this is the country. Outside the town there is no speed limit—at least not one that is enforced—and, even though the roads are in bad condition, most people drive at a hundred or more. Sergeant Griffin says the roads are too dangerous for such speeds and, to set an example, he sits on sixty.

'What's the urgency?' I ask, rubbing my eyes. 'And what's the time?'

'Don't know. Eight twenty-three.'

I haven't seen Sergeant Griffin since he turned up when I was sneaking around Bill's boatshed.

'Maybe he has found out what Bill's been up to,' says the Minnow.

'That doesn't explain why he would be in such a hurry,' I reply.

But the thought makes me anxious. I've been trying not to think about Bill. Now I realise I haven't prepared myself at all. The Minnow and I get out of bed and head for the shower.

I'm eating toast when Sergeant Griffin knocks on the door.

I can hear a small beeping sound—soft, constant, regular— as I walk through the backyard to the compost bin. I have a small colander of vegetable scraps and, even though I'm carrying it with both hands, bits of potato peel keep falling onto the ground. By the time I reach the bin I've dropped more than half.

'You afraid you might lose your way back?' asks Papa. It is a rhetorical question, so I don't bother myself with an answer. I like the word 'rhetorical'.

I lift the lid with one hand and tip the scraps on top of the seething mass of worms. Jonah's compost bin is nothing fancy, just an old plastic bin with a lid. The bottom has been cut out so that the worm castings enrich the ground below, but this has given the rats easy access. Exactly like our old one.

Occasionally Mum would ask Dad to fix it, but he was always busy with something else. One afternoon, Bill arrived with some chicken wire. He pulled the bin off the mound of rotting vegetable scraps, rodent-proofed the bottom of it with two layers of mesh, repositioned the bin and shovelled the decomposing mess back in. The whole job took less than an hour.

'No worries,' Bill said. Mum handed him a thank-you beer.

'You trying to get on her good side, mate?' said Paul Bunter.

Paul had been helping Dad with the truck's brakes.

'Reckon I am,' Bill replied, and Paul laughed.

Mum liked Paul. She used to say that of all Dad's friends, Paul was the easiest to talk to. The two of them would often sit and chat.

'Take no notice, Bill,' Dad said, as he walked up the steps to the veranda. 'I reckon I could die tomorrow and Paul would be first in the queue to take my place,'

Dad loved saying stuff like this.

'What queue would that be?' asked Mum, standing in the doorway, a six-pack under her arm.

'The Angie queue,' said Dad, matter-of-factly.

I love jam doughnuts. I prefer the hot-dog shape, rather than the round version, with real cream, not that horrible mock business. Sometimes I go to the pastry shop before I visit the pet shop. Mrs Blanket doesn't like people bringing food into the shop. She has a sign on the door that says *no food or drink*.

I buy my doughnut and walk across to the bus stop. There is no bus service at The Crossing. The government decided it was too expensive. But they left all the bus-stop seats. The one opposite Fielder's Pets and Supplies is green and grey and has a small bin next to it. Mrs Blanket donated the bin and it has the shop's logo on the side. I sit on the seat and open the paper bag. Bits of jam have stuck to the sides so I tear it carefully down the middle.

Today is the perfect jam-doughnut day. You can't eat jam doughnuts on the wrong day. Jonah thought this was a strange observation until I pointed out that the perfect day for pumpkin soup was overcast and cold, even better if it was raining. If you're wondering what the perfect doughnut day is, it's clear and sunny, but quite cool. And it's better if it is autumn rather than spring, so that there is a crisp feeling to the air. It makes sense when you think about it.

I finish eating the doughnut, wipe my hands on my T-shirt, and rummage around in my backpack for my pocket thesaurus. I don't usually keep it in my pocket, even though it is small enough to fit. The pocket thesaurus is a recent find. I bought it from the op shop behind the Lutheran church on Holly Street. The Lutherans pronounce it 'holy' as a bit of a joke. Ha ha.

The church is a simple wooden building painted buttercup yellow, and the parish residence, which is also painted yellow, has housed the Smith Family opportunity shop for as long as anyone can remember. It became a superstore after the flood. Clothes and toys arrived from all over the country and there are still quite a few unpacked boxes in the shed.

I paid forty cents for the Oxford Minireference Thesaurus. Minireference doesn't look like a word to me. I think it should have a hyphen between 'mini' and 'reference'. I mentioned this to Betsy Groot. She was watching me as

I left the shop with my purchase, so I felt I should stop and have a chat.

'Who are we to argue with a thesaurus?' she said when I told her about the missing hyphen. She had a point I guess. But I'm unconvinced. Plus, even though it is a mini-reference (I like using the hyphen) I'm not altogether sure I approve of the way some of its listings differ from the normal version. I realise it is short on space, but some of the entries are really compromised. For example, under 'crisp' it makes no mention of 'smart dresser' or 'fried to a crisp'. Crisp seems left a bit wanting. Yet it finds room to include 'pleat'—a word that doesn't get a mention in my full-size thesaurus. There are heaps of other examples, but I won't bore you with them.

I really want to get back to the boatshed. Something about the loft didn't feel right, and even though I've gone over and over it in my mind, I can't figure out what it is.

'C'mon in,' I said. 'Can I get you some toast?'

'Sure,' said Sergeant Griffin. He walked over to the tiny kitchen table and sat in Jonah's chair.

'Is this about Bill?' I asked. I felt my face flush, so I turned away and popped a slice of bread under the grill.

'No,' he answered. 'But if you had any information, you'd tell me, wouldn't you, Tom?'

I felt a trickle of water run down my legs.

'Sit down,' whispered the Minnow.

'I feel a bit odd,' I said. 'I think the toast will have to wait.'

'Now!' insisted the Minnow. I turned off the griller and sat opposite Sergeant Griffin.

'Sorry,' I said, 'but you do seem to have the oddest timing.'

Water continued to trickle. I hoped it wasn't noticeable.

'That's okay, Tom,' he said. 'I'm not that hungry.'

He leaned forward and patted my hand. 'But your Nana has had a turn. She's all right, but they've moved her to the nursing wing and she is raising hell. If you're up to it, she could do with a visit.' The news made me relax. Until that moment I'd had no idea how wound up I was over Bill.

'Is that why you were speeding?' I asked without thinking.

'Yes,' he answered. He looked at me strangely.

'What?' I asked.

'That was a clever question, Tom,' he answered. 'You should take up police work.'

'Just a good guess,' I said.

I stayed put while Sergeant Griffin phoned Dr Frank and explained the situation with my waters. If things weren't stressful enough, the Minnow was refusing to talk to me.

'It's not that I don't trust you,' I told her, 'but you're my responsibility.'

She was quiet as a mouse. 'I don't want to go back to hospital, either,' I said. 'But what choice do we have?'

Sergeant Griffin finished his call. 'Probably best that I take you straightaway,' he said. 'If you need anything, Jonah or I can fetch it later.' There was no room for negotiation. I hoped the Minnow was listening.

'You might want to grab a towel,' I said, and Sergeant Griffin's eyebrows shot up to his hairline. He collected a couple of towels from the bathroom and then helped me down the steps and into the police car. With both towels underneath me, Sergeant Griffin adjusted the seatbelt to fit comfortably.

I felt safe with Sergeant Griffin. Solid, dependable. And whether the Minnow agreed with me or not, right now I trusted him with her life.

We headed off. Sergeant Griffin drove at a steady pace.

When we arrived at the Mavis Ornstein Home for the Elderly, Hazel was waiting with a wheelchair. She took me straight to the nursing wing.

Dr Frank was on the phone, talking to Dr Patek. Every now and then he would look across at me and smile.

But it's a ruse. I'm still leaking.

~

By the time I see Nana it is mid afternoon. The nurse is on strict instructions that my visit be no longer than ten minutes. Dr Frank has warned me that even though Nana is quite distressed, I am to remain calm or the nurse will remove me. And I'm not allowed out of the wheelchair.

Dr Patek has advised total bed rest. Dr Frank is to monitor me over the next twenty-four hours. Hopefully the water stops leaking. They're worried I might go into early labour. I had to beg to see Nana.

'Thank you, Nurse,' Nana says in her bossy voice, 'but I wish to speak to my granddaughter in private.'

The nurse hesitates. She has been told to stay put.

'It's okay,' I say. 'Just come back when the ten minutes are up.'

The nurse doesn't look happy about it, but she wheels me over to Nana's bedside.

'Please, Tom, stay in the chair,' she says. 'And,' she turns to Nana, 'push the call button if Tom looks faint.'

'Of course,' says Nana. 'I might be old, but I'm not stupid.'

The nurse turns to leave, gives me what Hazel would call a withering look, then marches out of the room. She doesn't close the door.

'Oh darling,' says Nana, gripping my arm, 'you have to tell them to move me back. I can't stay here.'

'You'll be all right, Nana. They're just keeping you in for observation,' I say, all chirpy.

'No, Tom. You don't understand. I *can't* stay here.'

Nana looks like she's going to cry.

'What's wrong?' I ask her.

'I'm dying for a bloody gin and that's just for starters,' she says, and a laugh escapes.

For the first time ever, I realise Nana is frightened.

'Oh, Nana,' I say, 'push the call button.'

The nurse must have been loitering near the door because she rushes in almost immediately. She yells for assistance and I'm whisked off down the hall to a vacant room. Two orderlies lift me onto the bed while the nurse rushes off to get Dr Frank.

Poor Nana, she hates being alone. Which reminds me: I wonder what has happened to Papa? I haven't seen him since this morning.

At the Mavis Ornstein Home for the Elderly there is one hillside that gets a frost so thick that from a distance it looks like snow. It is at the far end of the property, about an hour and a half's walk from the chapel. Last autumn the frost came early. Papa collected me before breakfast. 'It's really cold, sport,' he said. 'Get your coat.'

Papa has an old bicycle. I always sit on the handlebars

because he straps his tool box onto the pinion at the back. Every time we ride together Papa tells me that I'm getting too big and that I should get my own bike. But I love doubling. There's a magic that goes with it.

Frost isn't anything like snow. For a start it is very fragile; if you try to move it, it disintegrates. For years, Papa worked on a snowman-shaped topiary hedge, but he lost interest when he could never get the frost to settle evenly. Now he prefers to build his frostman on the ground, mowing the shape onto the side of the hill a week or so before the frost is due. Sometimes the frost is early, sometimes it is late. Papa says timing is everything.

Nana has good reason to dislike the nursing wing besides the obvious fact that everyone who stays here is about to die or already dead. I don't like it either. I'm not allowed to get out of bed—even to pee—and I'm really hungry because I couldn't bring myself to eat the mush called lunch. If I had a phone I would call Jonathan and ask him to bring me something edible. But when I asked one of the nurses about it, she said, 'It's not a hotel.'

I wish Papa was here. 'That nurse is a bitch,' he'd say. 'I bet people die just to get away from her.' Okay, maybe that was a bit harsh, even for Papa.

I wish Hazel would visit. I could ask her to bring Nana's

gin and something for me from the tea trolley. Maybe I could ask her to give Papa a message.

'Hi, sweet potato.'

It's Hazel. She's standing in the doorway with a cup of tea and something on a tray. 'Hazel,' I almost shout, 'I was just thinking about you.'

'Well, are you going to ask me in?' she says, smiling. 'I come bearing gifts.'

Hazel watched as I ate three passionfruit scones. Mrs Fletcher's daughter, Ellen, brings them every second Tuesday. I've never had three.

The tea was cold but I drank it anyway.

'Thanks, Hazel. I was starving.'

'I can't understand why,' she said, nodding her head towards lunch, which sat untouched on the bedside table.

'Eating that would probably induce labour!' I said, hoping to get a response from the Minnow, but there is not a peep. I'm still getting the silent treatment.

'Oh, it's not that bad,' said Hazel.

But it was. Things were really bad.

Once, when I was six, I had a fit. Mum said I went blue and my body shook and my eyes rolled back. She said it was the scariest day of her life. She remembers screaming for Dad, who came running from the shed, took one look at me and told her to grab Sarah and the car keys. Then he picked me up and carried me to the car. He held me while Mum drove. I imagine he was scared but he never let on. Mum thinks I have no memory of that day and, for the most part, she is right. But I remember Dad's face. He never took his eyes off me.

'Hello kiddo,' says a man with a thin moustache.

'Hi,' I answer, but my voice sounds tiny, distant.

'You've had a bit of a turn,' he continues. 'Had your Mum and Dad worried.'

'I feel sick,' I say. It takes all my energy to speak.

'You'll be right,' says the man, laughing, but I didn't catch the joke.

I figure it's best to write Papa a note. Hazel's got her rounds to do, but she has promised to return after dinner.

> *Dear Papa,*
> *Please visit. I realise you're avoiding us but we need you.*
> *You know where we are.*
> *Love Tom. x*

I want to say more but Hazel will read it. And while she's willing to leave the note on the veranda for Papa to find, if I say too much she might think I'm losing it. Or, worse, she might try to contact Papa herself. He would hate that.

The middle of my chest feels tight and I know something's wrong. I keep pushing the call button but it doesn't seem to be working. I don't know what else to do. Maybe I should try yelling.

'You after some company?'

'What?'

'It's Peter. I was your stand-in chauffeur while Mr Whiting was away.'

'Oh, Peter, sure, I remember,' I say. I can feel sweat beading on my forehead.

'You want me to find a nurse?'

'I don't know,' I answer. 'How do I look? Do I look like I need a nurse?'

'You look okay,' he says and smiles. 'But you're holding the call button.'

I look at my hand. 'Yes,' I say, 'but I don't think it's working.'

'They're understaffed,' says Peter by way of explanation. Then he walks into the room and across to the only chair. 'Mind if I sit?'

I watch as he picks up the chair and moves it closer to the bed. I realise he is waiting for an answer. 'Oh, sure,' I say. 'Take a seat.'

He sits down, smoothes his trousers and carefully folds one leg over the other. He does this with the grace of someone who has practised the movement.

'How's your uncle?' I ask.

'Brother,' he answers. 'Marcus.'

'Sorry, that's right. How is he?'

'Good. No change.'

Shit.

I'm not sure what to say next. So, instead, I return the call button to its place under my pillow. Peter removes small pieces of lint from his trousers.

'You hardly seem old enough, if you don't mind me saying,' says Peter, breaking the silence.

'What?' I reply.

'Well, unless you're hiding your age extremely well, you've got to be at least fifty years younger than everyone else here.'

'Oh,' I say, relieved more than anything. I thought he was about to lecture me on teen pregnancy. 'My waters are leaking. They're worried I'm going into labour.'

'Still...strange they've put you here,' he says, waving his hand to indicate the nursing wing.

'Yes,' I agree. 'Last time they whisked me off to West Wrestler.'

'Marcus was there for a while. I had him moved here as soon as he was stable.'

'I was in the women's hospital.'

'Oh,' he says, laughing, 'of course.'

~

Annabel and I are sprawled at either end of the tinny, lines cast, eyes closed. It is warmer than usual and we have both stripped down to our swimmers. I'm at the pointy end, one hand holding my line, dangling in the water. I'm just beginning to drift off when Annabel breaks the silence.

'How long are we supposed to wait?' she asks, fidgeting in her seat and rocking the dinghy. Small ripples pulse outward, heading for the bank.

I'm not sure how to answer. What I want to say is that it takes a while to learn fishing patience.

'Tell her you never really learn it,' says Papa, coming to my rescue. 'That you just get accustomed to the boredom.'

'A while longer,' I answer. 'Half an hour. Maybe an hour.'

'What did you say?'

I sit bolt upright, banging my elbow on the oar.

Instead of Annabel, Bill is leering at me from the other end of the dinghy.

'You were talking in your sleep,' he says. 'And who the hell is Annabel?'

'No one,' I say, rubbing my arm and trying not to let go of my line.

15

It has been raining heavily for three days. Jonah says it's already flooding at the inlet, and Sergeant Griffin rang yesterday afternoon to say that the main road to West Wrestler had been cut off.

I'm still leaking so they've hooked me up to a drip. They've moved me into Nana's room, temporarily. Poor Nana is still in the nursing wing and Papa—the bastard—refuses to visit her. Every time I raise the issue he changes the subject. My guess is that something over there has him spooked.

Jonah has brought Rumbly. Hazel says she can't see a problem; a few of the residents have pets. But I've just noticed Campbell sniffing around.

'I'm not sure Rumbly's safe,' I say to Jonah who's sitting on the edge of Nana's bed.

'I can take him back home with me if you're worried,' he says, looking over at Rumbly's hutch, which he and Jonathan delivered this morning. What he really means is, I should have thought about this earlier.

'I'm worried one of the cats might tip the hutch over,' I say, ignoring his tone.

'Really?' says Jonah. 'I don't know. It's pretty heavy.'

'The Minnow is still not talking,' I say, changing the subject.

'Should you be worried?' he asks.

'I *am* worried,' I answer. 'I think she's really angry with me.'

Jonah leans forward and puts his hand on my shoulder. 'You're doing everything you can,' he whispers. 'She can't be angry at you for that.'

'You don't understand, Jonah. The Minnow thinks it's an issue of trust.'

'You're right,' he says, taking back his hand. 'I don't understand.'

The year before last, there was no frost. Papa and I rode to the hillside almost daily, to check, but each time was a disappointment. I couldn't understand why it meant so much to him, but it did.

We still had fun. We played hide-and-seek and I-spy. Sometimes we played chasings, even though Papa never played fair (disappearing the second I got close, then reappearing further away).

One morning, when it started to rain, we huddled under Papa's raincoat and made up stories about what had happened.

In my favourite story, our hillside's frostman had met the love of his life. Her name was Este, she was a garden fairy, and she lived with her family on the eastern escarpment of the Mavis Ornstein Estate.

Papa says all fairies are governed by rules. For example, the tooth fairy is only active in the hours before midnight, the pumpkin fairy only works between midnight and three, while the garden fairy works tirelessly all day, from dawn till dusk, seven days a week.

There are several varieties of garden fairy, and Este belonged to the Royal Gentiana—commonly referred to as the Noble Blue. The distinguishing feature of the Noble Blue, the thing that separates them from the others and marks them as unusual, is that these fairies are visible—every single day—in the brief moments just before sunrise.

Courtship was slow. Este was very shy. But our frostman was patient.

He would hike each evening to her garden and wait, all

night, for a glimpse of her at dawn. Then he would return to his hillside. But it was a long walk, and by the time he arrived home it was too warm for the frost to settle.

This, we decided, was the best explanation for why, even though it was freezing and the conditions were perfect, the entire hillside was frost-free.

'You want to come fishing this arvo?' asked Bill. I had heard his truck pull up out front and I walked onto the porch to see what he wanted.

He was standing on the second step. About a metre separated us.

'No,' I answered. 'I want nothing to do with you.'

'Listen, you little shit,' said Bill, standing taller than ever and leaning in close so that I could smell his breath. 'I know what you're up to.'

He smelled foul. I was trying to think of an answer when he hit me, hard, across the cheek.

'What was that for?' I asked. A pointless question, really, because I knew.

'She's not responding,' says someone. I can hear faint beeps.

I rubbed my cheek. I felt dizzy from the impact.

I decided right there and then that I might actually hate Bill. Jonathan would say that I'd reached my tipping point.

'Do you want me to hate him, too?' asked the Minnow. But I didn't answer. Even though I wanted the Minnow to have nothing to do with him, I didn't think I could ask her to hate him.

Bill leaned forward and plucked the FishMaster from the go-cart.

'Hey! What do you think you're doing?' I demanded.

'What does it look like,' Bill sneered. 'I'm taking your fancy-pants gear to the inlet. You coming or not?'

Shit. Now I had no choice. Knowing Bill, if I refused to go he would probably tip everything into the creek and bring me back an empty tackle box. Just to spite me.

'Wait,' I said, almost pleading.

'No,' he answered. Triumphant.

Bill turned abruptly and strode away. He opened the door of his twin-cab and climbed in, threw the FishMaster onto the passenger seat and slammed the door.

'Bill!' I yelled. But it was too late. He started the truck with a roar and drove off towards the inlet, skidding on the gravel and leaving tyre marks on the drive.

In a way I was relieved. Part of me wanted to run my heart out, get to the inlet and stop the bastard. But the other part of me realised that there was no hope of running. Even if I were as fit as a mallee bull, I couldn't run with the Minnow. So I went back inside, finished my lunch, went to the toilet, made a honey sandwich, filled a bottle with water, grabbed a cushion, put everything in the go-cart and set off for the inlet. I walked at a slow and steady pace.

All I hoped was that Bill would have calmed down by the time I arrived.

'You took your bloody time,' called Bill, as I walked down the pier towards him.

'I'm pregnant, if you hadn't noticed,' I replied. So far, so good, I thought.

'You're in luck,' he said, indicating the bucket. 'The fishing's good.'

His mood had lifted. My luck was as shiny as a freshly minted coin. Believe it or not, that's not a Nana saying, although if you think about it, it doesn't sound like something Nana would say. No, it's one from Mr Greerman. Remember the old guy with the pyjamas? Mr Greerman's sayings are different and he doesn't usually explain them— except to say that they make sense if you've been in the war.

I looked in the bucket and there were a couple of decent-sized fish. Then I casually opened the FishMaster. Everything was there. Mostly undisturbed, too. I felt a wave of relief.

'What? Did you think I'd chuck it?' Bill asked. There was that edge again.

'Of course I did,' I answered. 'That's why I rushed here.'

Bill threw back his head and laughed. 'Here you go,' he said, handing me his line. 'Take this and I'll make a new one.'

I pulled the cushion over to the edge and sat down, dangling my legs over the side. It would be okay. I'd just bide my time for an hour or so and then tell him I had forgotten to leave a note for Jonah.

'Dad!'

'Hello sport.'

'Dad,' I repeat, because I can't believe it. 'I'm dreaming, aren't I, Dad?'

'Not really,' he answers.

'Then things must be pretty serious to get you inside this place.'

'You could say that.'

'Where is Mum?'

'Not far. She and Sarah are in the car.'

'I don't get it.'

'We took a vote. I'm collecting you.'

'That's a bit of a bruise you've got there, Tom,' said Mrs Blanket.

'Yes,' I replied. My cheek is blue and sore and quite swollen.

'Clare will be back in about ten, if you don't mind the wait.'

'That's okay, Mrs Blanket. Jonah is buying me a steak.'

The Minnow prodded me. I turned to see what she was so excited about and found myself staring at a brand-new display cabinet. It reminded me of one of Nana's highboys, but with the front missing.

'What is going in here?' I asked.

Mrs Blanket looked at me and raised her left hand in a sign that meant 'wait'. Her right hand rummaged among all the stuff on the counter until she found what she was looking for. 'There you are,' she said to the pamphlet. 'Tom,' she said, waving me over. 'Come and look at my new acquisition.' Only someone with a love of language would use 'acquisition'.

Mrs Blanket pointed to a picture of *phycodurus eques*, a sea dragon from South Australia. It had a long snout and strange leafy tendrils for fins. I wasn't sure if I liked it.

'What do you think?' asked Mrs Blanket.

'Wow,' I said. 'It is hard to believe it's a fish.'

'I know,' she said. 'Isn't it amazing?'

'Incredible for arthritis,' said Clare, coming in through the back of the shop. 'Shit, Tom. Do you want something for that shiner?'

'Jonah's getting her a steak,' said Mrs Blanket before I could answer.

'It is my cheek,' I said. 'Not my eye.'

'Waste of a steak then,' said Clare and marched off to the fish tanks. She returned with a handful of weed that looked remarkably like Mrs Blanket's sea dragon. 'Hold this to your cheek until it warms, then rest it for twenty minutes or so.' She caught my expression. 'You don't have a tank?' she asked, although it was more of an accusation than a question.

'No,' I answered.

Mrs Blanket and I stood silent, while Clare digested the news that I didn't keep fish. 'Okay,' she continued. 'Once it warms, cool it down in a dish of water then reapply. Do this three times, then throw the weed away. And don't change the water.' Clare waited for a response.

'Okay,' I said. I reached out and took the weed. 'Thanks, Clare.'

'No worries,' she said. 'The bruise will be gone by this time tomorrow.'

The bell clanged as someone entered the shop. The three of us turned to see Jonah holding a small brown butcher's bag.

'Well,' said Clare, 'unless you're bloody vegetarians, that looks like dinner.'

Rumbly is the sweetest. On cold lights I let him sleep with me and the Minnow. He is so little that I have to make a special bed for him. I roll an old towel into a circle. I put his heart pillow and his beanie in the middle so that he knows it is his spot.

He's pretty smart, so it didn't take long to train him to stay put. Occasionally I wake up to find him asleep on my pillow. But I don't mind.

Back when Dr Patek introduced the moderate-exercise rule, Hazel would check on me. I'm not sure why she did this—given that I saw her almost every day when I visited Nana—and it made me feel uncomfortable. Jonah said I was just being paranoid. My thesaurus doesn't have a listing for paranoid. If I wrote a thesaurus I would definitely list it: **Paranoid:** delusional, fearful, suspicious.

There was a knock at the door, so the Minnow and I pretended to be asleep.

Jonah answered it. It was Hazel. I could hear them talking.

I was about to get up when I heard Jonah laugh. It sounded like they were fine without me. Rumbly stretched and yawned. I scratched his tummy. He opened his eyes momentarily, almost as though he was checking where he was, then fell back to sleep.

Eventually Jonah tapped on my door. 'Hazel's here,' he whispered.

'Hi, Hazel,' I said as I walked into the kitchen.

'Hi, Tom. How are you feeling?'

'Good, thanks.' Maybe it was time to clear the air. 'Did Nana put you up to this?'

'Of course,' said Hazel. But there was something about the way she said it.

'Oh,' I said, as I realised she was pulling my leg.

Hazel's smile broke into a laugh. 'I care about you,' she said.

'Sorry, Haze,' I said. 'I'm an idiot.'

'No,' said Hazel. 'But dare I say you're acting a bit para-noid.'

Jonah looked away. But I knew he was smiling.

In three weeks, it will be the twenty-sixth; the Minnow's prediction. The leaking has almost slowed to a stop, the rain has eased, Nana looks like she's coming good, and Papa, well, he is still being a bastard, and the Minnow is maintaining her silence. Hazel says 'three out of five ain't bad' so I'm not complaining. Although on a more personal note, I don't know where they'll put me when Nana comes back. If I had a choice I'd like to be back at Jonah's. I miss the quiet. There is too much going on here, although much of it is a rerun. Betsy Groot has had the same conversation with me every day.

'Oh, hello, dear. Where's your grandfather?'

'Not sure Betsy. Have you checked the veranda?'

'You realise there's someone in my room.'

'Mrs Gladstone. I've met her. She seems nice.'

'Don't ever get old, Tom. You die and someone moves into your room.'

Exit Betsy, enter Papa.

'Betsy Groot was looking for you.'

'Don't tell her where I am.'

'That horse has bolted. I've already told her to look on the veranda.'

'Well, I'm not there.'

'Where should I tell her to look?'

'Oh. Okay. The veranda's fine. I'll make sure I'm there tomorrow.'

Ground Hog Day.

'Hi, Jonathan.'

'Hello, Tom.'

Jonathan smiles at me and walks over to look at Rumbly who is curled up in one of Nana's hats. Jonathan's face does a squiggie thing. I imagine that's the face he'll wear when he meets the Minnow: crumpled and soft and affectionate. It's strange though; it's a face so unlike his normal expression that I wonder what the Minnow will make of it. I'd ask her, but I have given up trying to mend things between us. Eventually she'll come around. She always does.

'Nana's doing well,' I say.

'So I hear,' he says. He scratches Rumbly's tummy. 'Hazel tells me you might be going home.'

'Really?' I say.

No one has told me.

'I'm sorry,' he replies. 'Maybe I've ruined the surprise.'

'If it *is* a surprise, you haven't ruined it. Did Hazel say anything else?'

'No.'

Even if she had, Jonathan is not about to compound his mistake. He's a stickler for protocol, and his slip-up just now is clearly troubling him.

'Don't worry, Jonathan,' I say. 'I'll act surprised when I hear the news.'

'Thank you, Tom.'

Jonathan continues to scratch Rumbly. Rumbly is making the guinea pig version of a purring noise.

'Tom, can I ask you something?'

'Depends.'

'Fair enough,' he says. Someone sneezes down the hall. The atmosphere in Nana's room is like something from a movie. All that's missing is the tick of a clock.

'This is none of my business,' Jonathan continues, 'although it could be.'

Well, there's a typically Jonathan Whiting sentence.

Lawyerly. Ambiguous.

'I have no idea what you're talking about, Jonathan, so you may as well get whatever it is off your chest.' In the movie I'd have told him to 'come clean'.

'It involves Bill Hamperton,' he says.

The room is completely still. Jonathan clears his throat. He stands and walks to the window. 'Bill is in trouble with the law, Tom. I have friends—as they say—in high places and Bill is in the kind of trouble from which there is little escape.'

'Have they found him?' I ask.

'Yes, Tom, they've found him.'

'Oh,' I answer. I never thought they'd find him. I thought he was gone for good.

16

Caleb Loeb and Jonah Whiting are an item. I didn't hear it from Jonah. I heard it from Caleb Loeb. He wrote a note. It wasn't meant for me, at least not directly, but he must have known that it would get to me eventually.

Dear Jonah, it said. *You are everything to me. Kiss kiss.*

He actually wrote the words 'kiss kiss', I'm not making that up.

'What's this?' I asked Jonah when a small piece of paper fell out of his jeans pocket.

'Nothing,' he answered.

'Then give it to me,' I said. Jonah looked embarrassed as he handed it across.

'Kiss kiss?' My voice an accusation. 'Who the hell writes

kiss kiss?'

'That's a bit harsh,' said Jonah and snatched the note out of my hand. He folded it in half and in half again, then tucked it back inside his pocket. He took his time, ignoring my stare.

'Are you going to answer me or not?'

'Caleb.'

I knew it, but somehow it still hit me like a slap.

'Caleb Loeb?' I could hear the screech rising in my voice. 'Kiss kiss from Caleb fucking Loeb?'

'No need to swear,' said Jonah.

'You're right,' I said, 'I'm sorry. Now get out of Nana's room.'

I fell asleep this morning, right after breakfast. I had a very interesting dream about Bill's boatshed. In the dream I was an animal, small and very close to the ground. Maybe I was a possum, or a bandicoot. I'm not sure what I was. It doesn't matter. What matters is that, as an animal, I was safe.

It was dark. Bill was digging one of his holes, and I was scruffing about in the bushes nearby. At first I thought I was alone. The night smells had me excited and I was off in my own little world—until I recognised something familiar. It was one of those weird dream moments where I found myself somewhere odd and couldn't understand how I got there.

I turned my head to locate the direction of the scent, and that was when I spotted Bill, about six or seven metres away. I realised that if he looked up, he would see me.

A small pit of fear began to grow. A branch cracked and Bill put down his shovel and reached for his torch. He shone it in a wide arc. The light landed on me, stayed for a moment, then Bill dropped the torch and carried on digging. I couldn't understand why he had ignored me, until I remembered I was in an animal body. Relief flooded through me like a drug. Part of me wanted to walk really close and flaunt my invisibility. But the part of me that knew Bill's unpredictable nature, that he would just as likely kill a small animal as let it go, chose to scuttle off in the opposite direction.

When I woke up, I realised the dream had shown me something. I was no closer to discovering whatever Bill was hiding, but I now knew that animals were no threat.

They wheeled Nana back to her room this afternoon. And they transferred me to Nana's wheelchair and parked me in the corner. Hazel stripped and remade the bed. Someone brought a vase filled with flowers from the kitchen garden, old Mrs Beakle brought Nana a chicken sandwich and a glass of lemonade, and Jonathan arrived with a set of crystal tumblers and a bottle of Tanqueray gin. Nana had been gone less than a week but, as very few residents go to the nursing wing and actually return, she was something of a heroine.

Halfway through Nana's second gin, Hazel arrived with the tea trolley, shortly followed by the Thursday Night Bridge Players—a group of women whose names all begin with the letter P. Mike Spice and a bottle of sherry were right behind them. Nana's room was getting crowded, but each arrival was met with a cheer.

By nightfall the celebrations had kicked up a notch, as other residents wandered over after their evening meal. Those who couldn't fit inside her room—or didn't know Nana all too well—sat outside on the veranda, talking and drinking.

The Minnow and I were going back to West Wrestler. When it came time for Jonathan and me to leave, Nana held out her hand for me to kiss.

A queen surrounded by her subjects.

'Bye, my darling,' Nana said to me, a bit slurry. 'Thank you for keeping my bed warm.'

'Bye Nana,' I said, leaning out of the wheelchair and hugging her close. She smelled so familiar. I missed her already. Jonathan squeezed Nana's hand, and the throng parted to let us through. We headed down the wide veranda to the ramp at the main entrance.

'Little wonder she hated the nursing wing,' said Papa as I wheeled past. He was sulking in a quiet spot, a fair distance from Nana's party.

'You're lucky she doesn't talk to you,' I said under my breath, 'because if she did, she'd definitely *not* be talking to you now!'

He knew what I meant.

Jonathan drove at a steady ninety. I was quite tired so I slept on and off for most of the trip. I was too groggy to answer any questions when we arrived, but Jonathan was amazing, demanding to see the person in charge and taking care of everything while an orderly wheeled me to my room.

A nurse showered me and put me to bed.

'Dr Patek says to get some sleep and she'll be by to check on you first thing in the morning.'

I felt safe. I was drifting off when I heard someone.

'That you, Jonathan?'

'Sorry, Tom. Didn't mean to disturb you,' he whispered. 'I'll see you in the morning.'

'Thanks,' I said, but he was gone.

Nothing much changes.

You love someone, they die. You miss them. You grow older.

Sarah is sitting on the end of my bed.

I know she's there, but I keep my eyes closed. I have to make her wait. We both know she deserves it.

She is still there the next morning.

'You're a moody shit,' she says, the moment I open my eyes.

'And you're not?' I reply.

'No. I'm dead, you idiot.'

'You think I don't know that?' I had forgotten how annoying she could be.

'Listen, Tom. It's not easy to be here. If you had any idea how hard it was you'd...well, you'd...'

'Still the wordsmith,' I say.

'Piss off,' she says.

'Piss off, yourself.'

This was going well. A year and a half and it was like yesterday.

I sat up and looked at her. I thought she would be exactly the same, but something about her was different. If I didn't know better, I would say she looked older.

'Should we start again?' Classic Sarah. Miss Clean Slate.

'No. Just tell me about Mum and Dad.'

Sarah sat on the end of my bed and told me about the flood, and how she had spent weeks looking for Mum and Dad and me. I was sad to hear that; I thought the dead just found each other. Sarah said she thought she was going to be alone forever, until she stumbled across Dad at Fowlers Hill.

'Fowlers Hill?' I said. 'Why there?'

'No idea,' she answered. 'But something strange happens when you die. You think you're in control, but you end up places you don't intend.'

I knew what she meant. Papa has talked about this stuff.

'So, how are Mum and Dad?'

Sarah stared at me. She definitely looked older. She stood up and smoothed her dress. I realised it was new. I was about to ask her about it when she sat back down, closer this time, and took my hand.

'Sarah,' I said. 'You're scaring me.'

'Mum and Dad are dead,' she said, in her serious voice.

'Oh, for Christ's sake, Sarah, I know they're bloody dead.'

She pulled back and was gone. It was so fast that I rubbed my eyes a few times in case they were playing tricks on me.

'Don't leave, Sarah,' I said. But it was too late.

'She'll be back,' said Papa.

'Papa! You almost gave me a heart attack.'

'Sorry sport.'

Papa sat on the small two-seater couch and slowly crossed one leg over the other. He cleared his throat as though he was about to speak, but instead he leaned back and folded his arms.

'You're sure?'

'Of course,' said Papa. 'She is very young. It takes a while to sort out stuff at her age.'

I looked at him with a face that said I needed more.

'Okay,' he said. 'She tried to explain how hard it was to find you. My guess is she is faced with some tough decisions.'

'Like?'

'Like trying to decide where she wants to be. It was easy for me; I wanted to be near your grandmother. But Sarah's got lots of options.'

This was way too weird.

On the drive to West Wrestler, Jonathan told me that he had booked a hotel room, rather than drive back to The Crossing in the middle of the night. So I'm not surprised, the following morning, when he pops in to check on me.

He looks fresh, clean shaven.

'Well, if it isn't Mr Neat,' comments Papa, as Jonathan enters the room.

It's too late to say something so, instead, I give Papa one of my looks.

'Don't worry,' Papa says, 'I'll get out of your hair. Anyway, I want to see what they've done to the park since the last time I was here.'

As Papa leaves the room, Jonathan moves across to the windows and opens the curtains. Then he settles in the armchair and we chat, mostly about Nana and how relieved we both are that she has bounced back.

During a pause in the conversation, I remember something. Jonathan had been telling me that they had found Bill.

'Didn't you have a question?' I ask him. 'You know… about Bill.'

'Oh, yes,' answers Jonathan. He looks decidedly uncomfortable. He stands, puts his hands in his pockets and walks towards the door. When he turns to face me the discomfort has gone; in its place is Jonathan Whiting QC. It makes me nervous.

'Bill Hamperton,' he says, his voice deep and clear, 'will go to jail. My concern is thus for your wellbeing and that of your child.'

'I don't understand.'

'I think you do, Tom. Bill is the father, is he not?'

'Is that the question?'

'Yes.'

'I don't want to talk about Bill.'

'Tom,' says Jonathan, as he walks towards me, 'I'm sorry to be so formal but this is rather difficult.' He sits on the chair next to my bed. He clears his throat. 'Normally I wouldn't ask you such a personal question. But Bill has money. Some of it is legitimate, some not. It is your grandmother's wish that I take action to secure what I can on your behalf.'

'Nana knows that Bill is the father?'

'Yes, Tom. She has always known.'

17

Mum visits me every day. I feel her sitting next to me when I'm asleep. Sometimes she stokes my hair, sometimes she hums. When I wake up, she's gone.

Music is floating into my room. I think it's coming from one of the birthing suites: a woman's voice, slow, sad. It sounds like something Dad would play. He used to play the guitar. He was self-taught. He would sit on the veranda, usually after dinner, and play late into the night. Sometimes he would sing and Mum would cry. She said he made everything sound sad. I miss falling asleep to the sound of Dad's voice. If he were here, he could sing to the Minnow and me.

Jonah has a small radio in his bedroom which he listens

to when he can't sleep. Once in a while they play a song that Dad used to sing. I imagine it is him, even if it's a woman's voice. Nana only listens to movie soundtracks. Her favourite is *The Lion King*.

The Minnow is moving. I place both my hands on my belly. I can feel her turning. 'I miss you,' I say, but she doesn't reply. 'They're putting up decorations,' I tell her, ignoring her silence, 'because we'll be staying here over Christmas. Jonathan has bought us a tree, and Jonah and horrible Caleb have bought fairy lights. The three of them will be here this Saturday to set it up.' I really thought the fairy lights would get a response. 'You've no idea how lucky we are,' I continue. 'Not everyone gets to have their own tree.'

I lay back on the pillow and pull the sheet up under my chin.

'It's okay,' I say. 'Once you're born, you'll be able to see what I'm talking about.'

'I know about Christmas.'

'You do?'

'Uh huh,' says the Minnow, in a voice that sounds like nothing has happened. It's a tad irritating. Tad means 'a small amount', but it is actually short for tadpole. Not many people know that.

'You haven't said boo for weeks,' I reply, 'and all you can say is you know about Christmas?'

I can hear the resentment in my voice, but as I lie there, staring at the ceiling, I can't get the smile off my face.

'The Minnow's back,' I tell Papa, who has been dozing off and on all afternoon, stretched out in the armchair, using the end of my bed as a footstool.

'Well, she couldn't have been far,' he replies.

'Yeah, I know.'

Papa yawns. 'I found some music for you,' he says, pulling himself up. He walks over to the TV and plays around with the controls, scrolling through the channels until he finds what he is looking for. 'I overheard one of the nurses talking about it,' he says. 'It is a bit like elevator music, but it's better than nothing.'

Music fills the room. Papa and I listen for a while. I fall asleep.

In second grade, I won the class reading award. It was presented to me by a Visiting Special Person: a nun from somewhere foreign. I can't remember what brought her to The Crossing. Anyway, she spent a whole month at the school: giving talks, reading from her journals and generally helping out. She was kind. I don't know what made me think of her just now.

Mum is stroking my hair. Soft gentle strokes across my

forehead from left to right. I can hear faint beeping noises, far away in the distance.

'She seems fine,' says Mum to someone in the room.

'Yes, she is definitely doing much better,' is the answer.

Good, I think. I'm doing better. Better than what, I don't know, but I don't seem to mind.

'When will you remove the tube?' asks Mum.

The tube? I try to listen for the answer, but I can't quite make out the words. Everything is foggy. Mum and Sarah are standing at the end of the sand spit. They're looking over at me but the sun is in my eyes and I can't quite see their faces. I try to call their names, but my throat is dry and the words don't form. Suddenly I'm exhausted. My arms are as heavy as lead, impossible to lift. This is it, I realise. I have no way of reaching them. I am up to my neck in sand, only my arms and head are exposed, and I'm sinking. I try to move my legs, but the weight of the sand is crushing my lungs, draining my strength. I try to lift my head, but it doesn't respond. My breath comes in small pants. Grains of sand start to fill my nostrils. I'm suffocating and there's nothing I can do.

Once when I was small, Dad took me skiing. I was only three. He and Paul Bunter had an army mate who owned a small cabin in the Southern Highlands, about an hour's drive from the snowfields. Mum and Sarah stayed behind; I'm not sure why, but I think it was because I was jealous of Sarah. Mum probably wanted some time to bond, without me interfering.

It was freezing outside, but the cabin was warm. It had sets of bunk-beds along one wall and an enormous fireplace along the other, which Dad and Paul kept stoked with huge logs, day and night. There wasn't much of a kitchen, just an old sink and a small table. We cooked sausages on the coals, and sometimes Dad made stew. We wrapped potatoes in foil and cooked them in the ashes. We ate in front of the fire, the three of us squeezed into the only sofa. Sometimes I sat on the rug. I would inch closer and closer to the hearth, until Dad said my face was so red I was in danger of getting a tan.

During the day, Dad and Paul went skiing. Sometimes I went with them, strapped to Dad's back. He held his ski jacket upside down and I put my legs through the sleeves. He buttoned the waistband of the jacket around his neck and tied the sleeves around his waist. I was snug-as-a-bug and I loved it. The air was icy-cold on my face, especially when we were flying down a hill. Once, when Dad and Paul wanted to trek further up the mountain, they left me guarding the pile of ski jackets. I must have snuggled in and fallen asleep, because I have a clear memory of waking up as they pulled their jackets out from under me.

—

No one warns you about childbirth. No one tells you that no matter how hard you try to stop it, it is happening with or without your consent. I went to the classes. Jonah and I did all the panting and hand-holding and counting. I listened to the mothers who had done it all before. I watched a disgusting movie. None of it helped. None of it prepared me.

'Annabel? What are you doing at West Wrestler?'

'Tom?'

'Yes,' I say.

'Hi,' she says, beaming at me.

I can't think what to say. Her beauty has me tongue-tied.

Suddenly we're standing at the end of the pier. The sky is cloudy and the water is choppy and dark. 'Hold my hand,' she says.

'What are you going to do?' I ask.

She doesn't answer. She has a firm hold of my wrist. 'No!' I shout, as I realise what's happening. But it is too late.

My body twists as it hits the water. A sharp pain shoots up my legs and across my back. I reach around, frantically searching the gloom, but Annabel has disappeared. Fear grips my heart. My lungs are filling. My body is being pulled under the pier. It is dark and foreboding. Dark green sedge-weed brushes against my face.

Sarah has her arms around my neck. She is holding tight—too tight—and her weight is dragging me further from the house. I can see small fish and bits of rubbish, but the water is so murky that it's difficult to tell if the fish are alive. My hair catches on something. The water is rushing past, but my tangled hair keeps me fastened to the spot. Something large hits us, a log maybe, or a fencepost. The impact loosens Sarah's grip and the floodwater pulls her away. I feel around for her. I try to call her. Sarah! Sarah! But I'm being pulled underwater, and the sound echoes in my ears.

The water is cold. Too cold. My body is shivering. I'm unable to get my breath, unable to focus. The current is relentless. My hair feels like it's being ripped from my head. Branches are flying past, things are banging into me. I'm gripped by a panic so fierce that, for the briefest moment, I almost succumb. Suddenly I feel something hard, solid, a rock maybe, and I push against it. I use the momentum to pull my hair free, wrench myself to the surface and take a gulp of air.

Pain is pulling at my body. I wish it would stop.

I open my eyes. I've been transferred to the birthing suite.

The room is not what I expected; just a bed and an adjoining room with a bath. There is a chair in the corner, one of those ugly recliner types. At the moment Papa is sitting in it. Soft music is playing; something wishy-washy, no doubt calming, but I think I'd rather something loud and unforgiving.

A nurse enters. She seems oblivious to my pain.

'How are we doing?' she asks, not looking at me. She lifts my wrist and feels my pulse. My pyjamas are soaked. My hair is wet. Bits of sedge-weed are dangling from my sleeve.

'I think I'd like to get in the bath,' I say.

'Okey-dokey,' she says, 'I'll get that started.'

She swans past Papa and into the bathroom and turns on the taps. She pulls towels and different bits and pieces out of a cupboard and places everything on a bench that runs along the wall. When she's done, she walks back over to me and places her hand on my arm. I imagine she thinks she's being comforting.

'Don't try getting in by yourself,' she says, patting me like I'm a puppy. 'I'll be back in a minute with the midwife.'

'I'll be off then,' says Papa, standing up and straightening the chair.

'Great.' My tone is sarcastic and I want to say more, but a contraction is building.

'I'm sorry, Tom, but this really isn't my thing.'

I try to answer, but I'm doubled over. Noise fills my head. I manage to sit up only to see that the bath is overflowing, water is halfway up the sides of the bed. I reach for the call button, press it again and again.

'Please, Mum,' I say, in case she's listening, 'I can't do this on my own.'

Someone takes my hand. 'It's okay,' says a woman's voice, 'you're safe with me.' I try to see who it is, but my eyes won't focus.

'I can't do this,' says my voice in a whisper.

'Yes, you can,' she soothes. 'Just relax and let your body remember.'

'No one's coming,' I say, handing her the call button.

The room is swaying. The bed is soaked. I can't get my breath.

Softly, and without much effort, I feel myself slipping away. I have the vaguest feeling that I might actually be drowning.

The bath was filling nicely by the time the midwife arrived. She took one look at me and called the nurse. When neither of them could reach me, they called Dr Patek.

They cut me open. I have a scar along my belly.

18

Mum taps me on the shoulder.

'Sweetie,' she whispers, 'time to get up for school.'

I'm already awake, but I roll over and moan and stretch.

I open my eyes and Dr Patek is looking at me from the foot of the bed.

'It was too much for you, Tom, and you upped and left,' she explains.

'I know,' I answer.

'Have you seen the Minnow?' she asks.

'Yes.'

'She's beautiful.'

'I think so too,' I say. The room is still. I try to move but everything hurts.

'Have you been out of bed yet?' she asks.

'I'm not sure. Everything is a bit of a blur.'

'That's okay, Tom, you've been through quite an ordeal.' She is clasping a folder against her chest. She takes a step closer, so that she's standing to the side of my bed. 'I'll be back tomorrow,' she says, alternately patting and smoothing the hospital blanket, 'and I'll talk to the nurse about getting you up and moving around.'

They're keeping the Minnow under observation for another twenty-four hours. Papa is probably at the nursery, staring at her.

My curtains are closed but the room isn't dark. I have no idea if it's day or night. I should have asked Dr Patek the time. And the date.

The Minnow looks like Dad. She has his dark olive skin and his eyes. I'm glad about that. I didn't want her to look like Bill.

Everyone says she has my mouth. I keep holding her up to the mirror and there it is: my mouth, in miniature. It's weird seeing a feature you're so familiar with on someone else.

We stayed at West Wrestler for most of January. Dr Patek wanted to make sure we were okay before we went home. There were a few complications. I'm not really sure what they were; it was just too much information. They tell you all this stuff when you're half shot with pain killers and hooked up to a drip. God knows how you're supposed to take it all in. But suffice to say we're fine now. Suffice to say; don't you love that? I got it from one of the tea ladies. Helen. Heavenly Helen, I called her. She had lots of quaint expressions. She fell in love with the Minnow and cried when we left. I promised to send her updates. I told her I would send a photo every month. I'm really hoping Nana buys me a camera.

Jonathan has done everything. I think I want to adopt him, but I don't have the heart to tell Papa. 'Jonathan, you're amazing,' I say, trying not to cry. He has filled my room at Jonah's with baby stuff: a bassinette, a change table, a beautiful baby wardrobe.

'Jonathan, you're *amazing*,' I repeat, this time with added emphasis.

'It's your grandmother,' he says. 'She wrote lists, and I just followed orders.'

'Don't be so modest, Jonathan Whiting. You're the kindest man I know.' I place the Minnow in her bassinette and give Jonathan a hug. I realise I haven't hugged him before. You've got to hand it to the Minnow; she changes everything.

'Oh my god!' I shout as I realise the tiny cot that was

Jonah's old bed has morphed into a double. 'Are you serious?' I let go of the hug and leap onto the bed.

'The bed was my idea,' says Jonathan, looking a bit embarrassed.

'Well, I think it's an excellent choice,' I say, mimicking Heavenly Helen, and Jonathan laughs.

'Come on, Tom. Your grandmother will be counting the minutes.'

'Oh, darling, bring her here,' says Nana, arms outstretched, eyes focused on her grandchild. Nana is in bed. Ever since her stint in the nursing wing, she spends most mornings in bed, sometimes not rising till after lunch. She hated it at first, said it made her feel old. But it seems to be doing her good. She looks rested.

'Oh, she's beautiful,' Nana says, cuddling the Minnow. 'And the spitting image of your mother.'

'Nana,' I say, 'she is nothing like Mum and you know it.'

'But she has your mouth, and I'm sure you got that from my Angie.'

Nana is holding the Minnow so close to her face, it's a wonder she can actually focus. 'I'm so happy I could bust a gut,' she says, pushing her nose into the Minnow's neck. I've never seen Nana so happy.

'Isn't she just the most perfect child, Jono?'

'Yes, Valerie, she most certainly is,' says Jonathan.

'I'm going outside for a bit, Nana. Can I leave her with you?'

'Of course, darling, take as long as you like.'

I lean forward and kiss the Minnow's forehead, then I kiss Nana's cheek. As I move out of the way, Jonathan moves in and sits on the edge of the bed.

I find Papa on the veranda. I take the seat beside him.

'She's beautiful,' says Papa.

'The Minnow? Or are you talking about Nana?'

His face crumples. 'I love her more than anything, you know.'

'I know.'

'I can't let go.'

'Then don't,' I say. 'Anyway, what's the point? There's nowhere you'd rather be.'

Old Mrs Beakle shuffles past. 'Hello, Seth,' she says. She ignores me.

'Poor old thing,' says Papa.

'Don't change the subject.'

Papa takes a deep breath. He exhales slowly. For the first time I realise how strange it is to hear a dead man breathing.

'Jonathan is a good man.'

'He's *amazing*,' I agree. But I've said it a little too quickly and with way too much emphasis. An imaginary baby mobile has filled the space between us. Mini speech bubbles are bobbing on strings, filled with words to describe Jonathan: Amazing. Good. Clever. Thoughtful. Kind. Lovable. Alive.

I hope Papa can't see it.

'You know he can never replace you in my heart,' I say.

'Thanks, sport, but this isn't about you and me.'

Okay. Glad that's sorted. Something like pain fills my chest.

'Would it kill you to admit she's happy?' I ask.

'Kill me. Very pithy.'

There's no listing for pithy in the mini-reference thesaurus. I can't say I'm surprised.

'She knows you're here,' I continue, ignoring his tone, 'and you know she loves you. She just can't stay *in* love with a dead man.'

'Always on point, Tom.'

'I'm sorry, Papa.'

'It's okay, sport,' says Papa, but his words are empty.

Neither of us can think of what to say, so we sit in silence until we hear the Minnow cry.

'Someone's hungry,' I say, getting to my feet. 'And, by the way, here comes Betsy Groot.'

'I'm going for a walk,' says Papa.

~

The faintest waft of honeysuckle gives Mum away. It hovers reassuringly around the bassinette. I'm certain the Minnow can see her. I catch her following someone with her eyes, and sometimes she giggles and pulls her knees up as though she is being tickled. I was sad at first. A few times I actually got angry, even jealous. But I don't worry about it anymore.

But it's hard.

I miss her.

'I won't keep her out too late,' Annabel says to Jonah.

Annabel is taking me night snorkelling. I slip my hand in hers and we walk in silence, only the sound of the gravel in our ears. We reach the pier and a shiver runs along my spine. So much Bill stuff.

'You're safe with me,' says Annabel.

I know I am. I have never felt so safe. And yet the fear grows.

'I can take you back if you like,' she says, 'we can try again tomorrow.'

This is about the hundredth time she has walked me here. I have never known anyone so patient. I begin to cry. She catches my tears in her hand and rubs them through her hair. It's the strangest thing.

~

Rumbly has taken to sleeping with the Minnow. I'm sure there are rules about guinea pigs in bed with babies, but they look so sweet together I don't have the heart to separate them. He always starts off with me, curled up in his beanie next to my pillow. But sometime between the two o'clock feed and dawn, he makes his way into the bassinette, and I usually find them snuggled together. Once they were spooning, although he is so little it looked more like a baby cuddling a soft toy. I really need a camera.

I can feel Jonah's impatience as I undo the chain and remove the little gold sinker. I realise it is no coincidence that it's heavy.

'I wish it was just from me,' says Jonah.

'Me, too,' I reply.

We're standing on the edge of the pontoon. Jonah has spent the day with me at Bill's boatshed, rummaging around. We didn't find anything of interest, but that wasn't the point.

'What would I do without you?'

'Oh, I don't know,' he says. 'Get bored, drop out of school…I can keep going.'

'Ha ha. Jonah the funny man. Who would have guessed?'

It is the last of the day. Tiny bits of light are flickering on the water. I give the sinker a gentle squeeze. I can feel it sitting in the middle of my palm, contemplating its fate.

'C'mon Tom, I'm growing old.'

'Sorry.' I reach down into the tinny for the FishMaster. I have a line prepared and I attach the little gold sinker just above the hook.

'Cabbage or worm?'

'Cabbage,' answers Jonah, handing me a small leafy blob.

'Maybe we should row out,' I say, 'so I can drop it gently overboard.'

'Get in then,' says Jonah. 'I'll row.'

We climb into the tinny, and Jonah takes us out into the middle. The sky is pink. A tiny breeze has picked up.

'I love you, Jonah.'

'I love you too, Tom. Now get on with it.'

I look over the side. It's a bit too dark to see any fish. I was kind of hoping to see Sarah. Then it hits me. I don't want to catch a fish with the Bill sinker; I just want to let it go. I grab the scaling knife.

'What are you doing now?' asks Jonah, an edge of frustration in his voice.

'Letting go,' I answer as I toss the little gold weight into Jessops Creek.

Annabel has *The Secret Language of Birthdays*: an enormous book that describes the characteristics of someone according to the day they were born. The Minnow, December twenty-sixth, is the Day of the Indomitable One. No kidding. I wish I'd known about this book when I was pregnant. I never would have doubted her prediction for a second.

'Annabel is a Piscean,' I tell Jonah. I have borrowed the book, and it is taking up most of the available space on our kitchen table.

'She is February twenty-sixth: the Day of Arousal.'

'So?'

'It says, "People born on this day have a great capacity to arouse others both emotionally and mentally."'

'So?'

'Seriously, Jonah, don't you think it's uncanny?'

'Only if yours is the Day of the Sucked-In Loser.'

'Nup. All yours.'

'I won't keep her out too late,' Annabel says to Jonah as we leave the house for the umpteenth time and walk through the dark to the inlet. The moon is almost full.

'You're different,' she says.

She's right. Something has shifted.

'I know. I can feel it too.'

'We're still going to take it slow,' she says. 'At any point you just tell me when you've had enough.' Annabel turns and leads me to the end of the pier. Then she hands me a snorkel and mask.

~

In my dream I stand on the end of the pier and, instead of diving in, I push off into the breeze and fly low over the water. My arms are out in front, palms together making a point, and every now and then my fingers skim the surface. Strangely, I'm travelling incredibly slow.

After the initial shock, the water is warm, amniotic. There's a rushing sensation as the air leaves my lungs and my skin takes over, extracting oxygen in a seamless motion. As I slip deeper into the dark, my eyes adjust.

The debris comes as a surprise. The creek floor is littered with wreckage. The closer I swim the more I recognise: a sign from the post office, a rusting rodent cage from Fielder's Pets and Supplies, an old tyre, a scooter.

My father's truck.

I glide closer. I try to open the door, but it is stuck fast. I swim around the other side, careful not to look through the windscreen. The passenger door is the same. The handle breaks off in my hand. I'm not sure what to do with it.

I realise there is nothing for me here.

'You may never find out how they died,' says Papa.

'Can't you tell me?' I plead.

'Death doesn't give me access to the truth, Tom. You know that.'

'But can't you go and check?'

'It was a dream, Tom. You're asking me to search for a truck in a dream.'

'Couldn't you try?'

'No, Tom. I wouldn't know where to start.

19

Martha and I have volunteered to clear the boxes from the op shop shed. The Minnow is asleep in her pram, and I figure I've got at least two hours before she wakes. It's a warm sunny day, and Martha has dragged each box onto the lawn. We've actually got a system; we go through each box one at a time. Crap in one pile, things for the Minnow in another, saleable goods in the third. The Minnow pile is looking a bit healthy.

Clare arrives. I have never seen her outside the pet shop. She looks pretty. 'Hi, Clare,' I say. 'Clare, this is Martha. Martha, Clare.'

Martha stands up and holds out his hand.

'Hi, Clare,' he says. 'Please call me Will.'

'Hi, Will,' she says, shaking his hand.

'Will,' I say. It suits him.

'Yes, Tom,' he says.

'Please call me Holly,' I say. 'But just for this afternoon. I want to see if it fits.'

I never saw Sarah again. But Papa says I probably did her a favour; that as hard as it was for her to find me, the pull to stay would have been enormous. Papa explained that even though he loves being here with Nana, it takes a lot of strength.

I thought about it, and I think I know what he means.

It's sad though. If I had known that was going to be it, I would have taken my time, dragged it out. I keep going over the conversation in my mind, trying to figure out what sent her away. Why would she swear and carry on as usual, then get all huffy and disappear just because I got impatient with her?

Papa says the disappearance thing might have taken her by surprise too, and that I shouldn't place so much emphasis on the actual events.

I'm so lucky to have Papa. Being dead gives him a completely different perspective.

'Oscar,' I say. 'Is that you?'

'Wait right there,' he says, and he swims out of sight.

I have been night swimming a dozen times since that first time with Annabel. This evening I'm on my own. The days are cooling; you can feel autumn is just around the corner, but the water is still warm. I've brought the FishMaster with me and the plan is to have a quick dip then catch something for an early dinner. Jonah is at home minding the Minnow. He's besotted with her. You should see the two of them.

School starts in two days.

I'm really nervous. After the flood, I missed most of year nine and all of year ten. The kids from my old class will be going into year eleven, but I've had to sit an exam to assure the Board that I'm able to cope with year ten. Thanks to James Wo, I won't have to repeat year nine. But it'll be weird. I always felt sorry for kids who had to repeat a year, even though, technically, I'm not repeating.

Jonah is going into year twelve. He was always one year ahead of me, now he'll be two. He says I shouldn't worry so much, that I'll be fine. But it's Jonah who'll be fine. When I asked him how he planned on juggling school with a baby, he just shrugged and said, 'Life is just one day at a time.'

Jonah is a machine. He can cook breakfast, have a conversation with me and rock the pram with his foot. He'll probably learn to burp the Minnow while he's studying. Me? I can't multitask. I have no idea how I'll cope.

Everyone is being very supportive. Nana and Jonathan keep telling me they're as happy as Larry to mind the Minnow every day (although Jonah and I think they would probably fall in a heap and it would be left up to Hazel). Anyway, I've decided that while she's so little I'll take her to school, at least while I'm still feeding her. They've set up one of the offices as a mini-nursery.

Oscar reappears. He spits something into my hand.

'Don't discard your past,' he says. 'Learn to live with it.'

I look at the little gold sinker. It's almost weightless under the water.

'I've missed you, Oscar,' I say.

'You don't have to keep it with you,' he says, sensing my apprehension. 'You could keep it in the carp tank. I'm sure Mrs Blanket wouldn't mind.'

'Hang on a second,' I say. I swim over to the steps, climb up onto the pier and walk over to the tackle box. I drop the sinker into one of the compartments. It'll be safe there until I decide what to do.

A small splash interrupts my thoughts. Oscar is a long way out. 'Wait for me,' I shout. And I take a running dive off the side of the pier and swim as fast as I can to catch up.

This May will mark the second anniversary of the Mother's Day flood. In honour of the people who were never found, there is going to be a ceremony at the town hall. In a rather surprising turn of events (that's how the local newspaper reported it) it has been suggested that small crosses be erected in the courthouse grounds. The courthouse was chosen because of its well-maintained garden. It also has a fountain which the council has promised to renovate. Jonah and I were sent a letter informing us of the proposal. Everyone who lost someone was sent the same letter.

'What if I don't want this?' I ask. Jonah is sitting opposite me. We have hardly spoken since the letters arrived.

'At this stage they're just tendering it for consideration,' he answers, sounding remarkably like his grandfather. 'I guess they'll wait and see what kind of feedback they get before they decide whether or not to go ahead.'

'What do you think?'

'I don't know,' he says. He taps the letter with his index finger. 'I think it's great they're fixing the fountain.'

God, he can be annoying. 'But what do you think about the crosses?' I ask, pulling him back to the point.

'Not sure,' he says.

There's no choice but to play along. So I shake my head, lift the letter, have another read. Sigh.

Neither of us speaks for at least five minutes.

'Okay,' he says, breaking the silence, 'I think it's awful.'

'Me, too.'

'We'll be expected to act as though everything is back to normal.'

'That's never going to happen.'

'And I can't bear the thought of Mum and Dad being reduced to a couple of crosses,' says Jonah.

'Ditto,' I say, even though my reasons are different.

I'm slowly getting used to horrible Caleb, although my gut still tells me he's nothing but trouble and that one day he'll break Jonah's heart. The Minnow likes him, but that's only because he shows her his funny side. And he bought her the cutest pair of booties. The Minnow has a mountain of booties thanks to Nana, but Caleb bought her a matching pair and she's quite taken with them.

Jonah and Jonathan and the Minnow and I are at the Mavis Ornstein Home for the Elderly. Jonah wanted to bring Caleb, but I put my foot down. Everyone's in the common room, having tea. I've snuck out for a moment to chat with Papa.

'Do you think I should give it to the Minnow?' I ask.

We're sitting outside in the garden. Papa's avoiding Betsy Groot.

'I think that little sinker was always meant for her,' he answers.

'Wow,' I say, a bit taken aback. 'Why didn't you say something earlier?' There's a hint of annoyance in my voice. I hope Papa doesn't notice.

'I never knew you had a problem with it,' he says, matter-of-factly.

'Well I did.'

I let that sink in. Papa says nothing.

'I have to deal with my past,' I continue, trying not to sound rehearsed, 'and Bill will always be a part of it.'

'Biologically speaking,' replies Papa, 'Bill's smack-bang in the present.'

'Well, that's one way of putting it.'

This is classic Papa and me.

'So the sinker is appropriate, then,' I say. It's a statement, but it comes out sounding like a question.

'You know it is, Tom.'

Nana finally bought me a camera. It takes movies and stills. I'm driving Jonah mad as the Minnow is almost twelve weeks old and, apart from a few cute happy snaps that Hazel took, none of her early stuff is on film.

'Hey, Miss Camera Happy,' Jonah calls to me from the kitchen.

'Hang on a sec,' I say to the Minnow. I walk to the doorway.

'Uh huh?' I answer. Jonah immediately adopts his on-camera persona—part Jonah, part cooking-show host. It is hilarious, and he doesn't realise he's doing it.

218

'We should take the Minnow to the tree house.'

We've been meaning to go for ages. 'Seriously, Jonah, you're the best. But it's just the three of us, right? We're not taking horrible Caleb?'

'Tom, you promised to stop calling him horrible Caleb in front of the Minnow.'

'Sorry,' I say. I turn away to hide my smile.

The Minnow laughs. Rumbly has climbed into the cot and is licking her feet. 'Hang on, Jonah,' I say. 'You have to see this.'

Jonah and I stand at the doorway together. I have the camera running.

'I bet the Minnow thinks we're her parents,' says Jonah, putting his arm around my waist.

'For sure,' I say. I turn the camera on us and lean my head on Jonah's shoulder.

The Minnow and I are eating lunch in front of James Wo's mural. Jonah is going to join us after his meeting with the maths teacher. It's a school day and kids keep stopping to say hi—to the Minnow, not to me. She loves it.

I think Mum is here, too. Right now the Minnow is making little hand movements as though she is holding onto someone's fingers. Watching her makes me realise just how hard it must have been for Nana all these years. She must have heard me talking to Papa a million times, but she has never said a thing, never asked me anything. I can't imagine such restraint.

Jonah arrives and plonks himself down next to me. 'Starving,' he says, and opens his lunch box. The Minnow lets out a little noise.

'Hi, baby,' says Jonah. He leans across to her pram and gives her a smile. She smiles back.

'You finished already,' Jonah says to me when he realises he is eating alone.

'Uh huh,' I say. Jonah is in the top maths class. I can barely add up.

'I had better feed the Minnow before the bell,' I say. Jonah doesn't answer. He is like an animal when he is hungry. For the next ten minutes, Jonah and the Minnow eat their lunch while I stare at James Wo's mural.

It is after midnight, and Annabel and I are walking to the inlet in time for the moonrise. The night is clear and perfectly still. I have never been swimming this late. As we walk along the pier, I notice Annabel isn't carrying any snorkelling gear. When we reach the end, she turns to face me and steps in closer, placing her hands briefly around my waist. I notice a stream of bubbles rising from her shoulders. Definitely blue. I want to say something, but the moment passes.

'It's time,' she says.

She holds out her hand. I give her mine. She smiles. My world fills. 'I won't let you go,' she says, and without another word she pulls me over the side.

The water is beautiful, clear, warm. 'Follow me,' says Annabel, and we dive deep into the inlet. I'm almost out of breath when she turns and points above my head. At first I think she is instructing me to swim to the surface, until she pulls, hard, on my arm. Again she points, more enthusiastically this time.

It's the full moon, orange and low on the horizon, but high enough to escape the trees on the eastern side of the inlet. It's wobbling on the current, huge and magnificent. But my lungs are screaming. I push away and race to the surface.

When finally I spot Annabel, she has made it to the far side—probably in a single breath—and she is waving at me. I can't help but be amazed.

The Minnow is still betting she's a mermaid.

Oscar says she's just a good swimmer with great lung capacity.

There are only two people who call me Holly: Martha who is really Will, and Mrs Haversham who is a bitch.

'Holly!'

'Holly Thomas!'

Mrs Haversham. I think I'll ignore her for a while longer.

The Minnow kept me awake most of last night. I'm not sure what was upsetting her, but by the time my alarm went off for school, it was me who was upset. Now I'm so tired, I don't see the point. I should have stayed home. Instead, I have my head on the desk and my mind out to sea.

I don't know how he did it, but Papa found Dad, and the three of us are deep-sea fishing off the *Coast of Mary*; the most beautiful fishing boat I've ever seen.

'It's a launch,' corrects Papa.

The *Coast of Mary* is a gleaming white *launch* with an aqua trim that runs in little stripes along the deck. At the moment she is rocking slightly, and if I look over the side I can see that she is also painted aqua below the water line. She's built for deep-sea fishing, which is quite different from the type of fishing I'm used to. For one thing, they don't catch the fish to eat, instead it's all about the hunt. That, and the size of the catch.

Everything on the launch is purpose-built. Some of the rods are fitted into the frame of the boat, with winches for hauling in the fighters. There are two large white chairs at the stern, with rod holders and foot supports and drink holders and neck rests. Totally over the top, if you ask me, but Dad and Papa are lapping it up: lines cast, a cold stubbie each and an esky full of reserves at their feet.

There is a lookout above deck—which is also the helm. I'm up there now. You can see for miles, and I haven't even tried the binoculars. I turn one-eighty degrees at the sound of Papa's voice. Papa is telling Dad something and the two of them peel off a laugh at the punch line. I turn back to the view. The breeze is light, there is not a cloud in the sky and, no matter which direction I look, there is nothing but ocean.

The Minnow is below deck, sleeping like a baby. I went to check on her earlier, but Dad caught my eye and shook his head. When I hesitated he winked. I think he knows that Mum is down there with her. Well, at least I'm getting to spend time with Dad.

'Lunch will be in twenty minutes,' says a voice.

'Fantastic,' says Papa.

I continue to stare at the view. In a word, it is mesmerising. I want to write that down as today's word, but I'm not sure where I put my notebook. It's here somewhere. I had it earlier; I was writing words that were similar but different, like launch and lunch. Now that lunch has been mentioned, I realise I'm quite hungry. I wonder if Mum will join us.

Someone is shaking my arm. I can hear the sound of a crowd, laughing. It makes no sense.

'Holly,' says Dad. I can't believe he has called me Holly. I'm about to reprimand him, but he has disappeared.

'She won't answer to Holly, Miss,' says a male voice belonging to the boy from across the aisle. Crap. I have fallen asleep at my desk. Not for the first time.

'Sorry,' I say, eyes still closed.

'Follow me,' says Mrs Haversham's voice.

Double crap.

Jonathan got rid of the rental and has bought a brand-new baby car seat. This one is cream (to match the Bentley's interior). I secure the Minnow.

The weather has changed. Rain clouds have blown up from the west—a bad omen. Jonathan waits for me to get settled. It takes ages. First I can't find my biology notes, then, once they're found, I realise I've lost my timetable. I empty everything out onto the seat. It's a mess. I need a system. Maybe a new schoolbag would help; one that has more pockets and compartments. Eventually I find the timetable tucked into my notebook. Then I take a deep breath and put everything back in some kind of order. Mess does my head in these days. I have to be especially orderly with my school stuff. I think it's a coping mechanism.

At last, I'm buckled in. Ready.

'You right to go?' asks Jonathan.

'Yep,' I answer, even though my readiness is obvious. 'Sorry.'

Jonathan drives me to and from school, most days. Jonah rides his bike. The Minnow and I used to catch the bus. It's any easy walk with the pram, and the bus stop is only fifteen minutes away. But then Jonathan started turning up, and then it became a habit. At first he used the drive as an excuse to get me alone to talk about Bill. He wants to take my case to the police. He says it is abuse, pure and simple. I'm not sure. I think he is right, but I don't think I want to dredge it all up. Everyone at school would find out. The thought of it makes me sick.

I'm exhausted. Luckily Jonathan isn't talking. Even the Minnow is quiet. Occasionally she makes a sucking noise.

'I have asked your grandmother to marry me,' says Jonathan, suddenly. I open my eyes to look at him, but he is staring at the road ahead.

I'm not surprised. It seems so natural, like it was always going to happen.

'What did she say?'

'She said she would talk it over with you.'

Nana's roundabout way of getting Papa's approval.

'Well, you know how I feel about you, Jonathan.'

'Thank you, Tom. It means a lot.'

The Minnow claps her hands. I turn to look at her.

Papa is sitting in the backseat, staring out the window.

20

Jonathan and I say nothing for the remainder of the trip. As we enter the grounds of the Mavis Ornstein Home for the Elderly, I notice that the hedge is looking worse for wear. At least it isn't brandishing a negative message. But, come to think of it, maybe that is exactly what it's doing.

Papa has disappeared by the time I get the Minnow out of her car seat. I have to find him, talk to him. If he feels betrayed, who could blame him?

Caleb Loeb has done a runner. I have to monitor my face. Constantly.

'He'll be back,' I say. Luckily the wind is blowing— to distract Jonah from the hollowness of my words. It is pointless saying I told you so. But part of me wants to shout it over and over. Instead, I touch Jonah's shoulder, rub my hand across his back.

Jonah fiddles with his watchband. It was his mother's watch. He found it in the shed yesterday morning. 'Look at this,' he had said, holding it by the buckle. Then he put it on. It was a significant find, but he had waited over an hour to show me. Jonah is like that. He took almost a week, once, to show me a cufflink. I can't imagine Jonah's father wearing the sort of shirts that required cufflinks, but what do I know?

Still, I thought it strange that stuff could just reappear, so long after the fact.

I thought it was Papa's doing.

'Not me, sport,' he said when I asked.

'Then, who?'

'Beats me,' was the reply. He caught my look. 'But I can ask around.'

'Thanks, Papa.'

Jonah's eyes are bloodshot. He probably hasn't slept a wink. I know things are bad because he isn't even chatting to the Minnow. Nana always says that if you're lost for words in a crisis, grab a pot and cook something. She says it gives you something to do and, while you're doing it, the activity is relaxing. I'm following her advice and making scrambled eggs and toast. I hardly ever cook, because Jonah is better at it, but he has been sitting at the kitchen table for over an hour and if I don't eat something soon, I'll fall over.

'Jonah,' I say, as he walks around me to the fridge. 'Things seem to be turning up.'

'Turning up?' he says, grabbing the milk and sitting back down at the table. It doesn't matter how many times I ask him to use a glass, Jonah drinks from the bottle. But right now I haven't the heart to get cross at him, so I watch while he empties a litre down his throat.

'Yeah,' I say, 'you know, your mother's watch.'

'That's only *one* thing,' says Jonah.

'Okay,' I say, 'but you have to admit, it's unusual. After all this time.'

'Yeah. So?'

Sometimes conversation is an art, and to get anywhere with Jonah when he's feeling down, persistence is the key. 'So,' I continue. 'I wonder if stuff might be turning up at mine.'

'Like what?' he asks.

'I don't know,' I say. 'Stuff.'

'And...'

'And,' I say, passing him a piece of toast, 'I want you to come with me to look.'

'We didn't see anything at the tree house.'

'True,' I agree, 'but we didn't look around. I'd like to go back and look around.'

'Sure,' says Jonah. He looks at the piece of toast in his hand and looks up at me. It is as though he has forgotten what to do next.

'Butter it,' I say, and I use my eyes to indicate where the butter is sitting, right in front of him.

'Sure,' he says. 'Okay.' Jonah grabs a knife and starts buttering. I hand him the second slice. 'I can't believe you're actually cooking breakfast,' he says, and he gives me the full-wattage Jonah Whiting smile.

His face is so pretty and his eyes are so kind. I wish, for the umpteenth time, that I had killed Caleb Loeb when I'd had the chance.

I was only three when Dad gave me my first car. My first and only car, as it turns out.

'Here, little squirt,' he said.

We were standing in the shed, and I was willing my eyes to adjust to the gloom.

'For god's sake, Lucas,' Mum said to Dad. 'The poor kid has no idea what she's supposed to be looking at.'

Dad lifted me up and swung me onto his hip, grabbed a large object off the ground with his free hand and walked us both outside. The sunlight was blinding but, as my eyes adjusted, I could make out a shiny red car. I stood, unmoving. The tension must have been excruciating.

'Put her in it,' suggested Mum. Dad obeyed. He lifted me up and guided me into the seat. He placed my hands on the wheel, then lifted each leg until both feet were resting on the pedals. For the next hour, Dad pushed me around the yard, coaxed me to pump my legs, taught me how to steer.

After lunch I was on my own. I got more adventurous. The driveway had a small slope running away from the shed. It ended in a dip and I would drag my feet on the ground, to help slow my approach. When Mum realised there were no brakes, she made me wear my gumboots. This was even better as it meant I could brake at the last minute, skidding to a halt in the dirt.

That little car and I became inseparable. When Dad was fixing his truck, I would pretend to fix my car. Sometimes he would prop it up on boxes, so I could lie underneath it and fix the drive shaft. But mostly I drove it in the house. I would get out of bed in the morning and drive to the kitchen for breakfast. I would sit in the car and eat lunch on the front porch. I probably would have slept in it—if I had been allowed.

The day came when I was too big to get my legs under the bonnet. Reluctantly I passed it on to Sarah who used it as a dolls' playhouse.

'Your father found that car at Bunter and Davis,' says Papa, when I ask him about it. 'He spent months fixing it up.

The mechanics of those little pedal cars were fairly simple. All he had to do was straighten the drive shaft and remove the rust. It was the panel beating and respraying that took the most time.'

'It was metal?'

'Yes, sport,' replies Papa, 'and it was a little beauty.'

Oscar is really adventurous. He says that leaving Mrs Blanket was scary at first, but once he got used to it, he could never go back to being a tank-dweller. In a way, I know what he means. As much as I miss Mum, Dad and Sarah, I love my new life with Jonah and the Minnow. I don't think I could ever go back either. It was a strange realisation.

'Have you given the sinker to the Minnow yet?' asks Oscar, during one of our late afternoon swims. Ever since he suggested I keep the sinker, he hasn't left the subject alone.

'Not yet, Oscar,' I say. 'I still feel uncomfortable about it.'

'Are you talking about the sinker, or Bill?'

This is the problem with perceptive friends. They take no notice of your camouflage. 'Can we not get into this now?' I plead.

The water is warm and dark. I just want to enjoy it.

'Bill is the Minnow's biological father,' says Oscar, playing the same record as Papa.

'I don't care to dwell on it.'

'No one's asking you to dwell, Tom. But for your own sake, you might want to give up suppressing the fact. It's taking too much energy.'

'I don't want to talk about it, Oscar,' I say, my voice rising involuntarily. 'Please, just drop it.'

'Okay,' he says.

We swim across the inlet to the dinghy, which is moored about thirty metres from the pier. It is Bill's tinny, but he has been unable to collect it since Jonathan lodged an AVO against him. He isn't allowed anywhere near the inlet or Jonah's house. He can't even go to the boatshed unless he has prior permission. Jonathan said that once charges are brought against him, he will probably go to jail. Until then, he is living in town, in a room above one of the pubs. It is nowhere near the pet shop or the pie shop, so I haven't got much chance of bumping into him accidentally. Even if that happens, Jonathan says I am to remain calm and walk away. Bill is not allowed to approach me or speak to me.

'Can I tell you something?' Oscar asks. We have finished our swim and I'm about to climb into the dinghy.

'Do I have a choice?'

'Sure, Tom,' he says, waiting until I'm comfortably aboard. 'On this, you most certainly have a choice.'

I wrap myself in a towel and lean over the side. 'Okay, Oscar,' I say. 'Spill the beans.' I brace myself for a lecture.

'You are the strongest person I've ever met,' he says.

That's it? I'm not sure what to say.

'I'll be off then,' he says, and he dives under the tinny and disappears. A moment later he surfaces, about ten metres away. 'I forgot to tell you,' he shouts, 'I'm visiting friends on the other side of the outcrop.' What he means is: it's safe to cast my line anywhere this evening.

'Thanks, Oscar.'

I dry off and pull on my tracksuit over my swimmers. The sun has dropped behind the trees and the inlet is cast in shadow, but the sky directly above me is still light, deepening to a deep red smudge in the west. It's probably only half an hour till sunset, meaning I've got less than an hour to catch dinner. But the conditions are perfect, there is almost no breeze, the water is calm—and within no time at all I've cast two lines off the bow and am readying a third. My feet are cold, even though the rest of me is warm, and I make a mental note to bring socks with me from now on. Then I sit back and wait.

A fish tugs on the line that is tied to my wrist. I must have nodded off. I open my eyes and get a fright to see that it's quite dark. I sit up and hurriedly pull in the line, but it's empty. The two off the bow are no different, although the bait has gone from all three. Rascal fish.

Nothing for it, but to pull up anchor and go home.

I'm almost at the pier when something catches my eye: a small flint of light, coming from Ponters Corner. I continue rowing, keeping my eyes steady, waiting for it to happen again. I'm about to give up, when I see it, brighter and closer, and, if I'm not mistaken, heading for the pier.

I row faster, not caring whether it's obvious or not that I'm in a hurry. If it's Bill, he knows all my moves anyway, so the important thing is to make the pier before him and get home fast. Thank god I've got Jonah's bike.

I'm breathless by the time I arrive home. The bike crunches along the gravel drive, and I stop peddalling, slowing to a stop at the back of the house. I lean the bike against the stoop, tiptoe up to the kitchen door and let myself in. Jonah looks up at me. 'Hi,' he says. 'Why so quiet?'

'I fell asleep in the dinghy. I've got no idea what the time is and I thought you and the Minnow might be asleep.'

'It's only seven-thirty,' says Jonah. 'I take it there's no fish.'

'Nup. Sorry. Rascals took the bait.'

'It's okay,' says Jonah. 'I made just-in-case soup.'

I feel safe, if a bit rattled, and head for the shower.

Bill won't come here. He is not completely stupid.

Jonathan, the Minnow and I are walking across the Mavis Ornstein car park when Betsy Groot almost runs into me.

'Tom, dear, I need to speak to your grandfather.'

Jonathan has stopped walking. I realise he is waiting for me.

'Tom, dear, it's *urgent*,' she says, almost shouting the last word.

'It's all right, Jonathan,' I say, pretending to fuss with something on the side of the Minnow's pram, 'I'll catch up in a moment.' Reluctantly he walks ahead.

I wait until Jonathan's out of earshot before I speak to Betsy. 'Have you checked the veranda?' I ask.

'He's *never there*,' she replies.

'What is it, Betsy?' I ask. 'Maybe I can help.'

'It's your grandmother,' she tells me in a measured tone. 'She has had another turn. It is a bad one this time, dear. She was calling for your grandfather.'

My heart does a weird lurching thing. 'When?'

'When what, dear? answers Betsy.

'Doesn't matter. Where is she?'

'In her room, dear,' says Betsy.

'Sorry, Betsy, gotta go,' I say, and start running.

My skin feels thick and heavy, like I'm wearing a coat of armour crossed with a wetsuit.

It's dark, but my nose tells me I'm in the boatshed. I recognise the familiar mix of sweat, machine oil and wood smoke, overlaid with the scent of something delicious, which I can't quite place.

I squeeze under the door and head outside. The food smell is coming from the woodpile at the end of the deck. I waddle over and burrow my way into a section of the stack. It seems relatively easy. Blocks of wood give way. Ants scuttle.

I head down the stairs and into the yard. I sniff around, decide on a patch of ground and mark the circumference with a scratch-line (about a metre-and-a-half long and a body-width wide). I then proceed to dig the whole section to a depth of about eight centimetres (waist-high in echidna terms). My front paws do most of the work, helped by my nose, which has a surprising strength.

When nothing turns up, I stop. After a bit of thinking time (spent walking back and forth along the length of the dig), I settle on a smaller section and resume digging, straight down. In less than ten minutes I strike something hard and metallic.

Complete excavation—of what turns out to be a long metal box—takes until dawn. There is no padlock. I open the lid:

Three rifles in separate calico bags.

One Leopold Mark 4 long-range rifle scope.

Five boxes of *RUGER .204/5mm calibre* ammo.

~

It is all up hill from the car park, so by the time I arrive at Nana's room I'm puffed and sweaty. At least the Minnow enjoyed the ride; she thought the whole thing was a game.

Jonathan's face is ashen. He nods to me as I try to enter the room. I can tell he has been crying.

'What happened?' I ask the nurse who is standing like a guard dog just inside the door.

'And you are?' the bulldog asks, stepping in my way and using her hand as a stop signal.

'Jonathan?'

'Let her in,' says Jonathan, his voice barely above a whisper.

'Down girl,' I say, as I push my way past.

21

Horrible Caleb has turned up at school and Jonah is acting like a complete imbecile.

'Don't,' I warn him.

We're eating lunch down by the creek, and I can see Caleb moving towards us from the northern side of the two bunya pines. I know from the shift in Jonah's attention that he has spotted him too.

'Don't what?' says Jonah, in a pathetic attempt at masking his anxiety.

'Don't lie to me, Jonah Whiting,' I say. 'You know exactly what I'm talking about.'

'Tom,' Jonah says in his pleading voice, 'I need to talk to him; I need to find out what happened.'

'I keep telling you what happened. He showed his true colours. He was just using you, Jonah. Now he's moved on.'

As we argue, Caleb gets closer.

'Tom,' says Jonah, turning to look at me, raising his voice a little. I imagine it's for Caleb's benefit who is only about ten metres away. 'Can you give us a second?'

'No, Jonah, I'm not moving.'

'Fine,' says Jonah, then leaps to his feet. I try to grab his arm but he is too quick for me. I'm feeding the Minnow, so I'm forced to watch, helpless, as my best friend bolts out of reach.

'Jonah!' I shout.

But he doesn't turn around.

Victory spills across Caleb's face as he witnesses my defeat. I can't believe it, but in every way that matters, Caleb has won this round and there's nothing I can do but sit and watch.

'Please don't do this, Jonah!'

A few year-nine kids stop what they're doing, turn and stare at me.

'What?' I say, but the anger in my voice is enough to make them back off. I feel so frustrated I could scream, but I know I'm powerless to do anything but wait it out and hope Jonah comes to his senses.

—

Jonah returned before the end-of-lunch bell, and he and I ignored each other for the rest of the day. When the final bell sounded at three-fifteen, I pushed past him and left without saying goodbye. As the Minnow and I barrelled down the corridor, the school secretary stepped out of the principal's office and almost collided with the pram. 'Just the person I wanted to see,' she said, and my mind did one of those frantic searches, trying to figure out why. 'Your grandfather called and said he wouldn't be able to collect you this afternoon. He said he is staying with your grandmother, that you would understand.'

'My grandmother is sick,' I said, not bothering to correct her about Jonathan.

'Will you be okay to get home?' she asked.

'Yes, we can catch the bus.'

As the Minnow and I waited at the bus stop, I alternated between worrying about Nana and stressing over Jonah. I was so preoccupied that I forgot to get prepared and everyone had to wait while I traipsed back and forth, getting the Minnow and the pram and my bags on board. No one helped. Usually I would care. But today, I couldn't give a shit.

On the way home, we passed Jonah on his bike. I strained my neck to look for Caleb, but he was nowhere to be seen. Nana would call that a small blessing.

When the Minnow and I arrived at our stop, I sprinted

home. I grabbed the FishMaster and left immediately for the inlet. I didn't leave a note.

An hour later and I was wishing I had thought about grabbing some food. My stomach was starting to growl.

'I can watch the Minnow if you want to go get something to eat,' said Papa.

'Papa!' I said, startled. 'You've got to stop sneaking up on me.'

'Comes with the territory, I'm afraid,' he said.

'Anyway, thanks for the offer, but I'm trying to stay away from the house.'

'Trouble in paradise?' he asked.

'Caleb Loeb.'

'Oh.'

Papa and I chatted for a while. He seemed to be at a bit of a loose end. I imagine Jonathan's making him feel superfluous. I love the word 'superfluous'. I heard it the other day but this is the first time I've used it.

Eventually, Papa left. Nothing was biting, so the Minnow and I packed up and headed off, too.

It is dusk by the time we arrive home. The Minnow is fast asleep and I feel a bit guilty that she has missed her bath and her dinner.

I don't want to make any noise—just in case Jonah has crashed on the couch—so I leave the pram at the bottom of the steps, carefully lift a sleeping Minnow into my arms, push open the front door and tiptoe down the tiny hall to our room. As wet as the Minnow's nappy probably is, I don't want to change her and risk her crying, so I tuck her into her cot, covering her with an extra blanket to compensate. I wait for a moment to check that she has settled, then sneak out of the room.

The kitchen looks exactly as we left it this morning. This isn't right—even for someone as domesticated as Jonah. There should be signs of the after-school feeding frenzy. But there is nothing.

I open the fridge. The pie from last night is missing. It seems as though Jonah arrived home and, just like I did, rushed out again as fast as possible. At least he had the sense to think of his stomach.

'Oh, well,' I say, aloud.

I turn on the kitchen light, fill the kettle and put it on. I walk outside and collect Rumbly from his hutch on the veranda. He is happy to see me and he snuffles up under my neck. I push him onto my shoulder and wait until he gets his balance, then I walk back into the bedroom and change the Minnow's nappy. She is dead to the world, so I give her a quick once over with some wet-wipes and change her into her pyjamas. The kettle starts to whistle as I'm tucking her in.

The kitchen feels different. Jonah and I hardly ever argue, and, even when we do we usually make up pretty quick. Today's disagreement has left a space between us. A better word would be 'chasm'.

While the tea brews, I make a cheese and tomato toasty. Once I've got everything ready, I sit at the table, trying my best to calm down. Nana says it is no good trying to eat when you're already full, and of course she is right; anger is ruining my appetite.

Rumbly licks my neck and makes me laugh. 'You little sweetie,' I say, pulling him off my shoulder and holding him out in front of me. 'So, Rumbly, what am I going to do about horrible Caleb?'

He doesn't answer. Of all the guinea pigs, I pick the mute one.

I break off a piece of toast and Rumbly gobbles it up. I pour a little of my tea into the saucer for him.

After dinner, I wash my plate and wipe the table. Then I treat myself to a really long shower. Usually our showers are quick, but tonight I ignore the rules and keep the water running. The fact that Jonah is not here to rap on the door gives me some satisfaction.

I climb into bed with wet hair. But I'm too worried to sleep, so, to pass the time, I think up various ways of getting rid of Caleb. Unfortunately, short of murder, I can't think of one that offers a permanent solution.

Eventually I decide that, seeing as I'm awake, I may as well do my homework. I get up, check on the Minnow and shade the cot with a quilt. Then I sit at my little desk in the corner and turn on the light.

I open my notebook and write today's word.

Chasm.

Dr Frank has bad news: Nana has had a series of mini strokes.

Jonathan hasn't left her side. He looks awful. Hazel has organised him a room, to save him driving home every evening. But even though he is happy to shower every morning and put on something fresh, he insists on sleeping in the chair at Nana's bedside. He looks thinner.

'Hi, Jonathan,' I say. 'Any change?'

'Hi, Tom,' he replies. 'They had to bathe her this morning. She'd be horrified.'

He is right; she would. That this should happen to Nana, of all people, is hard for me to grasp. 'What's going to happen, Jonathan?' I ask.

'I don't know, Tom. I don't know.'

'Cheer up,' says Hazel, breezing into the room with a cursory knock. 'You would think someone had died.'

Jonathan and I both turn to look at her. She looks straight at Nana.

'Morning, Valerie,' she says. 'Just ignore the party-poopers.' Hazel elbows Jonathan out of the way. 'Scoot, the pair of you.'

I notice she is clutching a plastic bag. Oh, god no. Nana is wearing nappies.

'C'mon, Jonathan,' I say. 'Let's give Nana some privacy.'

Jonathan leans over and kisses Nana's forehead, then follows me out. A second nurse enters the room as we leave. She closes the door.

There's no sign of Papa or Betsy, so Jonathan and I walk to the clutch of chairs at the shady end of the veranda and take a seat.

'Here, Jonathan, hold the Minnow for a moment and I'll get the pram.'

Jonathan does as he's told. The Minnow is wide awake and happy to go to him. It only takes her a second to work her magic and, as I walk to the common room, I can hear her giggling. No doubt Jonathan is pulling his squiggie face.

Jonah and I still aren't talking. It has been two days. At breakfast this morning we moved around each other like well practised dancers—quite a feat in such a small space—and every now and then I bumped into him on purpose. Thank god it's the weekend and the Minnow and I can visit Nana. I decide we should leave straight after breakfast as it's quite a long walk.

Annabel is waiting for us at the gate. She does this sometimes. I'm not sure how she knows when to arrive; I've never asked.

Her hair is wet and hanging loose down her back. She is wearing a T-shirt over her swimmers and a towel is wrapped around her waist. The back of her T-shirt is soaked and she is barefoot; a pair of sandals hang from the last two fingers of her right hand. She looks relaxed, beautiful. As I turn out of the drive, she smiles at me and falls into step. It is often like this. We rarely speak.

At the bend in the road, just before the gravel reaches the tarmac, Annabel squeezes my hand and I stop. She leans down and speaks to the Minnow, then turns to leave.

'Give Valerie my best,' she says. Annabel always calls Nana by name.

'Will do,' I answer.

As I enter Nana's room, the scent of honeysuckle is unmistakable. A nurse is sitting in the chair next to Nana's bed. She stands and straightens her uniform. Before I can ask if there has been any change, she nods a curt hello and heads for the door. I guess that answers my question.

Jonathan must be showering, so I have Nana to myself for a little while. I manoeuvre the pram and position the Minnow as close as possible. Then I walk around to the other side of the bed, turning the chair so that my back is to the door, and try to get comfortable.

Once settled, I reach for Nana's hand. She opens her eyes and looks at me. 'Hi, Nana,' I say. I feel a flood of emotion. 'I was going to say it's good to see you, but I hate seeing you like this.'

She opens and closes her mouth. Then she sticks out her tongue, runs it along her top teeth. I'm not sure if she is thirsty or trying to speak.

'Nana,' I say. 'You're freaking me out.'

Her eyes don't leave me. I stare back at her, waiting for her to say something, but the best she can manage is an 'ahhh'. Eventually she gives up and rests her head back on the pillow. She gives my hand the slightest squeeze. I squeeze back. It takes everything not to cry.

Minutes pass. I get up from the chair and climb onto the bed, snuggling down against her chest. I pull her right arm over and rest her hand on my face.

She smells like lavender soap. So familiar and wonderful.

'Nana,' I say. 'Jonah and I aren't talking.'

I stay with Nana until nightfall. The Minnow has had her

evening feed and is tucked up in the pram. Jonathan says he'll drive us home. When I object he tells me he needs to do some washing and get a fresh set of clothes, and he reminds me that Jonah's house is almost on his way. I'm relieved. I didn't fancy another walk home in the dark. I think Bill has been shadowing me. It's nothing I can put my finger on exactly, just a feeling. And I'm positive he was skulking around at Mingin's when I was there last Tuesday.

Jonah had been talking about fixing some cup hooks in the kitchen and I decided to organise it and surprise him. I hadn't been to the hardware shop with the Minnow and I'll admit I was feeling a bit nervous.

Mrs Peck wasn't happy to see me—or the Minnow— but I pretended not to notice and trotted down to fixtures and fittings, aisle three. There was a whole section devoted to hooks. As Nana would say, I was spoilt for choice.

I ended up choosing the white plastic-covered variety as I thought they would be Jonah's preference. They were also quite cheap.

Mrs Peck was waiting at the register, arms folded, impatient.

She looked awful. She had puffy bags under her eyes and her lipstick was running off into the creases around her mouth—bleeding, Nana calls it—and her cardigan was inside out.

I put the hooks on the counter and handed her a ten dollar note. As she gave me my change, there was a loud crash at the back of the shop.

Mrs Peck flinched.

I was about to say something sarcastic, but Mrs Peck looked straight at me and shook her head. It was the tiniest movement, but she meant for me to see it. Then she walked the Minnow and me to the door.

It was very strange. Mrs Peck has never done anything like that before.

I realised we had something in common.

We are both afraid of Bill.

Jonathan looks tired. He drives more slowly than usual, and I keep checking on him to make sure he is awake.

'Wasn't that cute when I popped the Minnow in bed with Nana for her afternoon nap?' I say, breaking the silence. We swerve to miss a pothole.

'They're bringing a specialist over tomorrow, to run some tests,' he says.

'Oh, okay.'

'I want you to know, Tom, that even though your grand-mother and I are not yet officially married, I will make sure she gets the best care.'

'Okay.'

'And I've hired a private nurse.'

'Yes, I met her,' I say, not sure where this is heading.

'They want to move her to the nursing wing,' he says. He turns to look at me, worry etched onto his face. 'You understand she can't go back there.'

I nod. Jonathan turns back to face the road.

'So,' he continues, 'I've informed Hazel to hire anyone she deems appropriate.'

'I see. Thank you, Jonathan.' He is an angel. I want to tell him this but instead I look out the window. No use rubbing salt in Papa's wounds.

We drive the rest of the way in silence. It occurs to me that Jonathan has known Nana longer than I've known her. I've never thought about that before.

'Thanks, Jonathan,' I say, as he pulls the pram up the front steps. I give him a hug. Jonathan hugs me back. I can feel his sorrow. Nana hangs between us.

'Will you be all right?' I ask.

'Will you?' Jonathan replies.

Neither of us knows the answer.

'See you tomorrow, then,' I say, 'and thanks for the lift.'

Jonathan does a little wave; a hand movement that says a whole sentence. The Minnow and I watch him drive away.

Pinned to Jonah's front door is a note from James Wo. Shit, shit, shit. I forgot all about our Saturday appointment.

> *Dear Tom,*
> *I heard about your grandmother. I completely understand that she's your priority right now. I will, of course, cancel our Saturday meetings if that's what you wish. Alternatively, I can meet you as per usual and then drive you to the Mavis Ornstein at midday.*
> *James Wo.*

It took more than a week, but eventually Jonah and I made up.

Don't ask me about Caleb. I can't bear thinking about him. Let's just say I'm confident there is no future, so I have given up worrying.

If you're wondering about my complete one-eighty, blame Oscar!

I had gone to the inlet for a swim on my own. I often do this when I wake early. Nothing matches a swim for clearing my head, and Jonah is always happy to mind the Minnow. They were both asleep so I left a note. Back in an hour, it said.

Oscar showed up. He can always tell when something is troubling me, so I told him all about horrible Caleb and my fears for Jonah's heart. I explained the rift between

Jonah and me, and that we weren't speaking.

Oscar gave me a crash course in reverse psychology.

I tried it out when I got home and it worked a treat. I told Jonah that I was sorry for being such a bitch and that maybe I had been unfair to judge Caleb so harshly. After thinking it through, I added, I was prepared to be open-minded.

Jonah looked so relieved, I actually felt bad about lying.

That evening, when the Minnow and I returned home from the Mavis Ornstein Home for the Elderly, Jonah confessed—over dinner—that he was having second thoughts about Caleb.

Oh, yes. Oscar is a total legend.

22

Friday the 26th of December. The Minnow's first birthday.

We celebrated in Nana's room, and I took lots of photos of the two of them together. I'm not sure Nana knew what was happening. It was so sad, seeing her like that. I kept thinking how different things had been twelve months earlier, when she had returned, jubilant, from the nursing wing. The Minnow's party was sedate by comparison.

On Saturday the twenty-seventh of December, at 11.34 am, Nana died.

Hazel handed me a print-out of Nana's 'last hurrah' that afternoon. 'If I seem a bit abrupt,' Hazel said when she saw the look on my face, 'then I'm sorry.'

'O..k..a..y,' I said, drawing out the word. 'She has been dead, what, three hours?' This was not what I expected.

'Sorry,' said Hazel, and she turned and walked back into the common room.

'That was weird,' I said, aloud.

'Don't worry, dear,' said Betsy Groot, who had materialised in front of me. 'Hazel is an absolute pet, and she grieves for us terribly when we pass.'

That made sense. 'Thanks, Betsy,' I said, but she was gone.

I walked to the end of the veranda, hoping to find Papa, but the place was deserted. I sat myself in the rocker and began to read Nana's instructions.

Nana wanted to be dressed in her whites and buried with her favourite bowling ball. Her favourite photo—the one taken when the Great Eight won the District Champions Trophy—was to be placed on the coffin and given to Jonathan after the service. She had paid in advance for a celebrant. There was to be no religious rubbish. The service was to be brief yet personal.

Luckily for the Minnow and me, on the Saturday that Nana died, James Wo had a dentist appointment at eleven-thirty, so he dropped us off at the Mavis Ornstein Home for the Elderly an hour earlier than usual.

When the Minnow and I arrived, Jonathan was giving Nana some water. I stood at the doorway for a moment, watching him go through the ritual.

It was a painstaking process, taking almost an hour to get Nana to drink just half a glass. Jonathan would repeat the exercise four times a day.

He winked at me as the Minnow and I walked over to the bed and I kissed first Nana, then Jonathan, on the cheek.

'How's she doing?' I asked, knowing the answer.

'Great,' answered Jonathan.

'Gigi,' said the Minnow, as I lifted her up and plonked her on the bed.

'The Minnow's here,' said Jonathan, leaning forward, gently brushing Nana's cheek with the back of his hand. No response.

Jonathan resumed the water ritual. 'How's that, Valerie?' he asked, tipping a fraction more into her mouth. 'I bet that feels good.'

'It'd be better with a bit of gin in it,' she replied.

Her first words in four months.

Jonathan and I looked at each other and burst out laughing. The Minnow joined in. When we looked back at Nana, she had died.

Jonathan is devastated. I'm not sure he'll know what to do

with himself after the funeral. He has spent every moment of the last four months at her bedside. The poor thing still wanted to marry her, but seeing as she couldn't speak, it seemed wrong. Besides, Nana hadn't officially accepted his proposal.

Jonah is staying with his grandfather. He might stay for a while as we're worried about Jonathan being alone.

Papa, on the other hand, is being really cagey. I want to know what will happen next, but he refuses to discuss it. I get the feeling that he and Nana will disappear after the funeral, and it is really pissing me off that I'm going to lose both of them and he won't even talk to me about it. I've asked Oscar for his thoughts, but he is no help. Says it is none of his business.

Jonathan is the executor of Nana's will.

'Everything is yours, Tom,' he says. He is looking better, if a little too thin. 'I will have her savings transferred to your account if you let me know your bank details.' Jonathan shuffled some papers. We are sitting in his study. It's all brown leather and bookshelves. Jonah describes it as old-school masculine.

Jonathan cleared his throat. 'It will take a few months, but eventually her room will be reassigned and her bond will be returned. It's over two hundred thousand, Tom, and you will have access to it when you turn eighteen.'

It was a lot to take in. Two hundred thousand. And change.

I've always wanted to say that.

I'm sitting at Jonathan's desk. Jonathan's study door is half open and I can see Nana and Papa sitting on the couch in Jonathan's living room. They're holding hands. Papa looks happy, content. He has aged thirty years.

Nana looks sad and tired and a bit stressed. God knows why they're here—probably Nana's weird sense of etiquette, and, knowing Nana, I bet she is wishing Papa wasn't quite so attentive.

The Jeffrey Gallico Chapel is crowded. Nana was popular. Bowls players from clubs as far away as West Wrestler and Banyaban Creek have made the journey. All of them are dressed in their whites. There is a collection of trophies at the front of the chapel. Each one bears Nana's name, with some of the wins going back decades.

Friends are taking turns to speak. The bowls players tell funny anecdotes. Eventually it is my turn.

'My Nana was one of the most amazing people I've ever met.'

I hadn't rehearsed or written anything down. I had

cried so hard on Sunday that I figured I would be able to get through my speech without a hitch. Now, I wasn't so sure.

I looked around the chapel. It was hard to tell who was dead and who was alive. Some of the guests were sitting on the laps of others and there was some loud complaining. But what could I do?

'When my family died, Nana saved my life,' I said. 'She was strong and no-nonsense and loving and kind and sympathetic. She knew and safeguarded all my secrets, she watched over me and trusted me to survive—even when she disagreed with my choices—and she loved the Minnow and me with all her heart.

'One of the saddest things is that the Minnow will never know *my* Nana. My Nana wasn't that old woman, stuck in bed against her will, unable to speak. My Nana was a champion bowls player, a royalist, a gin drinker, an ex-smoker, and a loyal friend. Most of all, she was funny and full of life and I will miss her forever.'

I turned to the front row. 'Nana was saved from the nursing wing by a kind and wonderful man, Jonathan Whiting. And, while her last months weren't what she would have chosen, Jonathan made them bearable.' Jonathan is sitting next to Jonah and the Minnow. He is crying.

'We love you, Jonathan,' I said. 'And Nana loved you too.' I had to say it. Papa would just have to understand.

~

I throw my things into the dinghy and climb aboard. I pull on the oars and the tinny glides away from the pier. I steer towards Ponters Corner, keeping my ears tuned for Oscar's familiar splash.

I'm not disappointed.

'Hi, Oscar,' I call over the side.

'Tom,' he answers, popping his head out of the water. 'Ready?'

Oscar has promised to take me to Banyaban Creek. It's too far for me to swim, so I'm following him in Bill's dinghy.

About an hour later, we round the last corner and I get my first glimpse. I haul the oars into the tinny and let the current pull me along. Banyaban Creek is Oscar's favourite spot and he's been promising to bring me here for months.

I can see why. It's mysterious and dark and incredibly beautiful. The trees on either side are enormous, with branches so broad and foliage so thick that they touch in the middle, forming an arch. It feels like we're moving through a cave.

'Tie up to the stump,' says Oscar, breaking me out of my trance. I look across to where he is pointing and, sure enough, there is a large stump jutting out of the water about ten metres ahead. Once alongside I secure the dinghy with the rope.

It's cold in the shade, and I understand, now, why Oscar insisted I borrow Jonah's wetsuit. I strip off my shorts and T-shirt and start pulling it on. When I'm ready, Oscar reappears. 'Did you bring everything?' he asks.

'Yep. Snorkel, goggles, underwater torch, flippers,' I answer.

'Okay, Tom,' he says, 'kit up and follow me.'

I pull on the flippers, lean over the side, wet my goggles, spit on the lenses to prevent them fogging, adjust my snorkel. Oscar pops his head out of the water. 'The torch,' he says. 'Bring the torch.'

I check everything, grab the torch and jump over the side.

The water is dark, and it's almost impossible to see, but I don't want to use the torch. I'd rather wait until my eyes adjust. Besides, Oscar's silvery scales flicker constantly and it's an easy swim with the flippers and the current. Ten or so minutes later, Oscar turns and stops. 'Okay, Tom,' he says. 'Time for the torch and a big breath.'

The torch casts an eerie light and suddenly I'm grateful for the flippers because I can keep pace with Oscar who is swimming fast and deep. The water is green and murky and strangely familiar. My torch flashes on something red.

Dad's truck.

'It's okay,' says Oscar. 'This is why you're here.'

I shine the torch through the windscreen, but it is too murky to see inside. I move around to the driver's side, pressing my face to the glass, my heart pounding, my lungs screaming.

The cabin is empty.

Time's up.

I push hard against the truck and kick with everything I have left. My right hand clips something, knocking the torch from my grasp, and for a frightening moment I lose all sense of direction, blind in the gloom.

'It's okay,' shouts Oscar. 'You're almost there.'

A moment later my head breaks the surface. I lean back, gulping air, moving my aching arms and legs in slow dog paddle, just enough to keep me afloat.

'You wanted to know,' says Oscar, bobbing up on my left.

He is right of course. Oscar's always right.

I'd had nightmares imagining Dad trapped in his truck, caught in the seatbelt, unable to get free, helpless as the engine conked out and the flood waters rushed in.

But what I didn't know—what I hadn't realised until now—was that finding Dad in the truck was my greatest fear. Not because I'm squeamish, I'm not, but I have to believe that Dad tried to save us. If I had found him just now, I wouldn't know what to think.

Life. It's the weirdest thing.

'Thank you, Oscar.'

'No worries, Tom.'

It is three weeks since Nana died.

Jonathan is inconsolable, and Jonah stays with him most nights. On the bright side, Jonathan's house is brimming with casseroles and orange cakes and scones as all the (elderly) women in his neighbourhood rally around. Jonathan Whiting is a bit of a catch, it seems.

It is January and the school holidays are in full swing. The weather has been really hot for the past two weeks, so Jonah and I devised the holiday-cool-down-plan. It's very simple: every morning Jonah arrives after breakfast and the three of us wander down to the inlet for an early swim. Then we mooch around at home, reading, playing with the Minnow, sleeping. By late afternoon we walk back to the inlet and swim until dusk. Sometimes I catch dinner. Jonah cooks. Then Jonah cycles over to his grandfather's and I read the Minnow a bedtime story.

I haven't told Jonah yet, but a few days ago, while I was making a cup of tea, I thought I heard the Minnow. She was having her afternoon nap, so I tiptoed into her room to check on her. She was fast asleep, teddy scrunched under her arm. The room was hot and stuffy so I walked to the window and opened the curtain to let in the breeze.

As I turned around I caught sight of someone leaning across the Minnow's cot. She was wearing a dress I didn't recognise: orange and pink check.

I knew it wasn't Nana.

'Mum?'

'Tom,' the woman answered. She turned and faced me, smiled.

She looked younger, a bit sadder maybe.

'I've missed you, Mum,' I said, as I walked into her outstretched arms.

We hugged. Tight and hard and for a long time.

I couldn't believe how good it felt.

Acknowledgments

To David Pollard for his boundless love, belief and support, and for everything in between. I couldn't have done it without you.

Siboney Duff for flagging my story as YA, for her manuscript appraisal and advice, and for her faith in me. Sib, you're a legend.

Tristan Bancks for his feedback and encouragement. Louise Holdsworth for her attention to detail.

Cassidy Light, Danika Cottrell, Sam Whortlehock, Jessie Cole, Nil Alemdar McHugh, Elisabet Mangsten, Petra Sweeney, Sam Toomey, Denise Greenaway, Lynne Casey and Sally Brakha for reading the early drafts.

Jakk Armstrong for always being there.

Jane Pearson for being the kind of editor writers dream about.

Katie Harnett for the beautiful cover illustration.

Finally, to Michael Heyward, Anne Beilby, Imogen Stubbs, Jane Novak, Stephanie Speight and everyone at Text for welcoming me to the family—oh, and for changing my life!

Thank you.

DEC - - 2015